TAKEN BY THE MAJOR

AN AGE GAP VALENTINE'S DAY ROMANCE

AVA GRAY

❀ Created with Vellum

ALSO BY AVA GRAY

CONTEMPORARY ROMANCE
Harem Hearts

3 SEAL Daddies for Christmas

Small Town Sparks

The Billionaire Mafia Series

Knocked Up by the Mafia

Stolen by the Mafia

Claimed by the Mafia

Arranged by the Mafia

Charmed by the Mafia

Alpha Billionaire Series

Secret Baby with Brother's Best Friend

Just Pretending

Loving The One I Should Hate

Billionaire and the Barista

Coming Home

Doctor Daddy

Baby Surprise

A Fake Fiancée for Christmas

Hot Mess

Love to Hate You - The Beckett Billionaires

Just Another Chance - The Beckett Billionaires

Valentine's Day Proposal

The Wrong Choice - Difficult Choices

The Right Choice - Difficult Choices

SEALed by a Kiss

The Boss's Unexpected Surprise

Twins for the Playboy

When We Meet Again

The Rules We Break

Secret Baby with my Boss's Brother

Frosty Beginnings

Silver Fox Billionaire

Taken by the Major

. . .

Playing with Trouble Series:

Chasing What's Mine

Claiming What's Mine

Protecting What's Mine

Saving What's Mine

The Beckett Billionaires Series:

Love to Hate You

Just Another Chance

Standalone's:

Ruthless Love

The Best Friend Affair

PARANORMAL ROMANCE

Maple Lake Shifters Series:

Omega Vanished

Omega Exiled

Omega Coveted

Omega Bonded

Everton Falls Mated Love Series:

The Alpha's Mate

The Wolf's Wild Mate

Saving His Mate

Fighting For His Mate

Dragons of Las Vegas Series:

Thin Ice

Silver Lining

A Spark in the Dark

Fire & Ice

Dragons of Las Vegas Boxed Set (The Complete Series)

Standalone's:

Fiery Kiss

Wild Fate

BLURB

I didn't need anyone to rescue me from my miserable life, not even an ex-military major who walked into this small town looking like he owns it.

There's something about Tate.

His confidence borders on arrogance, and I couldn't peel my eyes away from his muscular biceps when I first saw him. He, too, stared at me with an invisible drool.

But Tate and I could never be together. He's rich, with a property he just inherited in town.

And me? Let's just say I manage to care for my little sister while being broke.

There's nothing glamorous about my life, especially with my late dad's best friend constantly harassing me.

Tate felt like the source of more problems when I first met him, but he's slowly becoming the man who would protect me and my sister.

He just doesn't know that there's another tiny addition to this family.

A baby who will look just like him.

1

TATE

I sat in my office, chair leaning back, focused on the ball I lobbed into the air. Up and down. Catch, toss. Catch, toss. It wasn't as if I had ever had grand plans to be a ball player, or was even invested much in the sport, but one of my men had given it to me, and he had. It had been all of his hopes and dreams, all wrapped up in rubber, twine, and leather.

"I want you to have the ball if something happens," he had said.

"Ain't nothing going to happen," I said with all the confidence in the world.

I had to be confident. Nervous leaders made for nervous men. I could be confident. I wasn't going out on that patrol.

Not everyone came back.

Calvin Huntington had been his name.

Toss, catch. Toss, catch.

Back home, I kept that ball with me as some kind of reminder, a token of lost dreams and misplaced hubris. Today, it was none of that.

Today, it was an old baseball and something to occupy my mind, so I didn't think.

I didn't feel like using my brain this afternoon. I had already burned it out by reviewing the documents from my father's estate. I had a never-ending pile of them. Insurance companies were appearing out of thin air wanting proof so they could divest themselves of their money and give it to me. Medical bills for treatments I didn't know the old man was getting were grabbed from money I didn't even know I had access to.

And communications from multiple lawyers. I had banks I needed to follow up with. There were accounts that needed managing. Properties that needed upkeeping or divesting. Belongings to sort, employees to pay. I didn't want to think about it. I wasn't sure how I was supposed to deal with it from half a continent away.

I had no fond memories of tossing a ball around in the back yard with my father. We never bonded over teams or spent long, hot afternoons at the ballpark eating hot dogs and waiting for our team to hit a home run. But I had this ball, and it had been infused with Huntington's wishes. Maybe they spilled out a little bit each time it took to the air.

"I see you're busy."

I didn't shift to see my first lieutenant giving me lip.

"Mind your own business, or I'll bust you for insubordination."

"Your door is open, so I am taking that as an invitation," he said as he stepped in and parked his ass across the desk from me. He sat and watched as I tossed the ball over and over.

I ignored him and his lack of official decorum. Manners be damned, I outranked him. "Show your superior some respect."

"With all due respect, Sir, when was the last time you took leave?"

I caught the ball. It smacked into my palm. I looked dead into First Lieutenant Gardner's eyes.

"A real leave, Bowers. One where you can sit on a beach, drink beer, fraternize with the opposite sex," he continued with a flinch from my glare.

I chuckled. "Are you telling me I need to get laid?"

"If the boot fits, lace that bitch up and kick some ass with it."

"What do you want?" I finally asked.

"Colonel Manning wants to see you in his office."

"Why didn't you say so? If he chews on my ass for being late—"

"He won't. He said if I run into you." The emphasis was on the 'if'.

With a grunt, I relaxed back against my chair. It wasn't exactly comfortable, but at the moment it was about all I had the mental fortitude to deal with. "Did he happen to mention why?"

"He did not." With a heavy exhalation of a long, weary breath, Gardner pushed himself back onto his feet. "Door open or closed?"

I stared into the empty hallway for a long moment. Fuck it. I set the baseball on my desk with a thunk and pressed up to my feet. "I'm coming."

I didn't feel old. I just felt tired, but the knees bitched at me as I stood. First the knees, then the back. I blamed the chair.

"Major," Gardner said with a hint at a salute as he turned one way down the hall, and I turned the other way toward Manning's office.

The sergeant, seated at the receptionist desk outside the colonel's office, snapped a quick salute as she saw me.

"Is he in?" I asked.

"He's expecting you."

I knocked on the frame of the open door. Manning had his back toward me. His office had a real desk—unlike the folding table that served in my temporary office—and shelves covered in manuals. His desk was piled with file folders on one side and a computer on the other. And his chair looked like real upholstered leather.

My salute was lazy at best when he turned and waved me in.

"Major Bowers." Colonel Manning's voice rolled like booming thunder.

"Sir?"

"Sit down, Bowers."

I sat.

He opened a file folder and read over whatever the paper inside told him. He did that for a long while. His expression was dour. Questions started to move about in my head. Nothing so vigorous as a bounce, more like a meander from random thought to random thought. Was I being reassigned? Where to? I really did not want to go overseas again, and I sure as hell was not looking forward to being deployed.

"What are you doing here, Tate?"

Oh, fuck. Manning used my first name. He only did that when something was sizable. The first and the last time he had called me Tate was when he told me my father had passed away.

"Sir? You told First Lieutenant Gardner to send me your way if he saw me."

Manning shook his head. "That's not what I meant. Why are you still here? Why haven't you retired yet?"

I shrugged. "Nowhere else to be, Sir."

"That's bullshit, and we both know it. Your father died."

"And I took bereavement leave," I pointed out.

"You did, and then you came back. You've inherited a sizable chunk of change, Major. So, why did you come back to push pencils around a folding table of a desk?"

I shrugged. "What else was I supposed to do?"

"I am sorry you lost your father, I truly am. But why would you want to hang around here when you now have the freedom to do whatever it is you want? That's not a situation everyone is granted."

"If you were in my boots, would you?" I asked. I really wanted to know.

Ever since I attended the funeral, I had been walking in a cloud of fog. Thinking took effort. I wasn't sad. At least, I didn't think I was. I hadn't spoken to the old man for a long time, had no idea he was even sick. He could have said something, but he never called me, either. To say we had a contentious relationship put far too much emotion into whatever it was we had. There was an obligation of family between us, and that was about it.

I didn't feel the drive to do anything. Should I stay in the Army, or should I retire? If I retired, what the hell was I supposed to do then?

Colonel Manning leaned back and toyed with a pen and its cap. "When I was a kid, maybe eighteen, nineteen, there was this cherry red Camaro down the street from my mother's. Nineteen sixty-nine with twin black racing stripes across the hood. It was a classic even then. Spent most of its time up on blocks. But I knew when I got the chance, I would get myself one of those cars."

He focused on the pen and the cap for a moment in silence.

"Did you ever get your car?" I asked.

He nodded. "Uh-huh. When I was about twenty-five. I kept it for four or five years. It ran for maybe six months the entire time I owned it. It was a money pit on wheels. Every single valve and seal, every tiny piece of rubber trim had to be replaced at great cost." It still sounded like he loved that car, even if it was taking all of his money.

"Why are you sharing this with me?"

He tossed the pen on the desk and sat up straight. "Because, if my daddy left me half the money I know you inherited, I would walk out that door" —he jabbed his finger at his office door— "and go find myself another nineteen sixty-nine cherry red Camaro and drive it into the sunset. And probably, straight to an auto-parts store. The point is, there is something out there that has your soul, and you know the means to find it and reunite with that part of yourself."

"So your soul is a bright red American muscle car?" I had no idea what my soul was. Any chance of discovering what it might have been was taken from me by a father who thought discipline and order were the way to a life worthy of living.

"Maybe my soul is a red sports car. It is driving fast and the eternal dream of youth in jeans and leather jackets. It's the idealization of the long drive across a desert highway and milkshakes at the next rest stop."

I chuckled. "Your soul sounds a bit like some movie from the nineteen fifties. Something with James Dean and Marlon Brando. Or maybe Marilyn Monroe."

"That might be a little before the right time, but you've got the idea. Something perfect and unattainable. Tate, you need to go out there and attain for those of us who can't. Find your soul, live a dream life. Retire."

2

KENZIE

few months later...

AThe shopping cart had one flat wheel. Why did I always end up with the cart with the wonky wheel? I walked slowly down the aisle for no other reason than I was tired and I didn't want to fight the cart any more than I had to.

A large red and pink wall of fake fur blocked my vision before I identified an oversized Valentine-themed gorilla settling into the cart. I sighed as I reached for it and hauled it back onto the shelf.

"You do not need a stuffed animal bigger than you," I said.

"Spoil sport," Ruby complained.

"Do you need a class pack of Valentine's cards?"

"What? You aren't going to make me make them this year?" she quipped.

"Excuse you, you made them? I'm pretty sure I'm the one melting the crayons and putting them into the heart molds. Everyone always loved your heart-shaped crayons. Every single one of your teachers always made sure to mention them."

Ruby rolled her eyes. "They just said shit like that because they knew you couldn't afford the store-bought cards. How come you are willing to buy them this year?"

The truth was, I didn't have the money to buy them this year, but I was also running out of time. "Language. No time."

"Well, I don't need them this year. They stopped having us do all that mandatory Valentine's Day stuff in the sixth grade."

I stopped the cart. "Good. Hey, I made crayons for you last year. Why didn't you say anything then?"

Ruby shrugged. "You were having fun. Besides, my friends are weird and love them."

I wasn't having fun. I did them so she could participate like the rest of her class.

She pulled another stuffed animal off the shelf. "Can I get this one? Kenzie, look at its eyes, so big, so cute."

It kind of looked like my sister with big green eyes, a tiny nose, and lips a little out of proportion and on the big side. It was cute, but Ruby was cuter. Not that I'd ever tell her I thought so.

"So, no Valentine's cards?" I asked. I didn't try to hide the relief in my voice. I didn't remember elementary school as being so much work when I was the one in school. And middle school had just been a blur of dodging bullies, doing math homework, and Mom dealing with a baby. I certainly didn't remember Mom ever having to do nearly as much schoolwork as I did for Ruby.

"No cards. Can I have this?" She found yet another stuffed animal.

I groaned. "No, Ruby, you cannot."

"But you don't have to buy class cards. This is only"—she checked the tag— "five bucks," she whined. It was a fake whine, but my exhaustion was real, so her attitude was grating on my last nerve.

"We don't have five bucks."

"If you don't have five bucks, why are we even in this store? Come on, Mom, you're not being fair."

I stopped and closed my eyes. Damn it, our petty banter had caught someone's attention. And odds were good that someone was staring at us. Ruby only ever called me 'Mom' when it would fluster someone or really tick me off. I didn't have the energy to deal with either situation.

"If Daddy would only pay child support. But I guess he can't from Folsom. Stupid prison system."

I stayed there with my eyes closed and tried not to laugh. If Ruby had gone as far as talking about her 'daddy in prison,' someone was being too nosy about our business.

I opened my eyes and looked around. I caught some middle-aged lady giving me a side eye. I didn't know who it was. The half of town that knew us would have started laughing at Ruby's *Daddy in prison* comments. Ruby and I didn't have parents. Technically, we were orphans. And it still hurt, but we had gotten to the point in our grief that we could crack jokes. At least Ruby had.

Biologically, Ruby was my baby sister. A big surprise to my parents when I was almost twelve. Up until that moment, I thought I was going to grow up an only child. Legally, I was her appointed guardian. As her responsible adult, I fell into the job of 'Mom'.

"Come on," I groaned. "I want out of the Valentine's aisle sooner rather than later."

"I thought you wanted to look at the Valentine's stuff."

"No, I hate all this lovey-dovey hearts crap," I answered. "I came down this way because there were no people."

"Is that why you don't have a boyfriend?" Ruby asked.

"What?"

"You just said you don't like this lovey-dovey stuff. Boyfriends like this kind of thing." She held up a pair of hugging monkeys. I remembered wanting a toy like that when I was younger. They had magnets in their little hands that kept them holding on to their partner. One was red, the other pink. Their little noses were heart-shaped, and they probably had little embroidered hearts on their chests.

I snorted. "Boyfriends have nothing to do with this sort of thing. And if you get one who does, that means someone had to tell him to go to the store and buy it. I keep telling you boys are stupid." I started to walk a little faster.

"Is that why you won't let me date?"

I froze, absolutely froze in place. "What? You don't date." I couldn't believe what I was hearing. Ruby didn't like boys. She thought they were icky and had said so more than once. Oh, God, I wasn't ready for her to hit full-blown puberty. Not yet, please not yet. My voice was shaky. Boys were going to be interested in my sister sooner rather than later. She was cute, and she was going to have serious curves. She was already trying to hide her developing chest behind baggy shirts. "Are you even old enough to be talking about dating?"

"I'm practically an adult," she retorted.

"You're thirteen. Who asked you out on a date?"

"No one. Not yet. But you are always saying that I'm never going to be allowed to have a boyfriend, that I have to focus on school…"

I let out a sigh. "I guess if you want to date, we can discuss the details when we come to it. Do you want to date boys?"

Ruby shrugged. "Not particularly, but it seems like more and more kids at school are. How old were you when Mom let you start dating?"

I shrugged as we turned the corner and I continued to head toward the back corner of the store.

"Mom never really gave me rules like that."

"Dad?"

"Same. I mean, I went out on one date once. He took me to a movie, and Mom and her girlfriends were going out that night and they ended up at the same movie."

"Uh, that sounds horrible. Where was Dad?"

"At home with you. It wasn't as bad as it could have been, I guess. Mom threw popcorn at us all night. But I didn't really date much." And by much, I meant at all. One awkward date in the ninth grade, and that was it.

I stopped again, this time in front of the feminine hygiene products.

"Oh, that's why we're here," Ruby groaned.

"Grab what you think you'll need," I said as I made my selection.

"I have stuff at home. Can I spend my money on the monkeys instead?" Ruby started.

"We don't have money for stuffed animals because we need money for this, every month. And I have to buy quarters for laundry," I explained.

"How do you know we don't have money for those monkeys?"

"It's called budgeting. Maybe I should teach you. It sucks to learn all of this stuff the hard way."

She tried to put her choices into the cart as if she weren't actually doing it. Her attention was off down the aisle, and she dropped the

17

products into the cart as if I wasn't watching. So much for practically being an adult. I fully understood the awkwardness and embarrassment. She wasn't really ready for the biology that came with being an adult, even though she had to deal with it. I said nothing, and we moved on as if nothing had just happened.

Ruby rushed ahead and grabbed a bag of heart-shaped chocolates from an end display. I didn't say anything when she dropped those into the cart. When she noticed I left them in the cart, she tried putting something else in, a box of heart-themed Band-Aids. I quietly lifted the box out and set it on the shelf.

I put a small bottle of cheap shampoo in the cart. Ruby eyed it.

When my attention was on the selection of conditioner, she must have taken the shampoo out, since it was gone when I put the conditioner in. This had somehow turned from a shopping trip into a personal challenge. I grabbed the shampoo and dropped it back into the cart. If I stopped paying attention, not only would the hugging monkeys end up in the cart, but she would also probably find a kitten and put it in there too.

The last item she tried to sneak in was a round hamster-looking stuffed creature. It was covered in hearts. It was cute and I hated pulling it out of the cart. I wished I could give Ruby everything she wanted and was keenly aware that I couldn't. I was beginning to hate everything about this shopping trip.

Ruby held up a bottle of soda. "Can I at least have this?" The label had some Valentine's promotion printed on it.

"Why is everything covered in hearts?" I complained.

"That's a no?" she asked.

"You can have the drink. I'm just sick of everything being covered in hearts right now."

"That's because you're some kind of love Scrooge. You hate Valentine's Day."

I opened my mouth to protest, but she wasn't wrong. I really did not like February fourteenth, and it had everything to do with love.

3

TATE

L ight filtered through the dirty windows. Dust motes filled the air. It made me think of some overly dramatic or romanticized scene from a movie with light made visible in rays spreading into the room. It was neither dramatic nor romantic. It was cluttered and dirty.

I left an orderly, structured, and organized life for this? Retirement wasn't exactly what Colonel Manning had described. I had no hot rod car to drive off into the sunset with. I had no soul to connect with. At least, none that I had found yet. What I did have were several properties scattered up and down the California coast and dotted in major cities across the States and an apartment in Paris.

I could only imagine they were all semi-neglected like this one was. Well, all accept the house in Chicago, the one I had lived in before getting shipped off to boarding school. The one Father had lived in until he had to be put into the hospital.

That property was the easy one to deal with. I paid someone to clear it out and auction it off. Everything inside it went away without my ever having set eyes on it. I didn't need to visit for nostalgic reasons. I didn't have good memories of the place.

But this one, a late-Victorian style home with a detached barn, had intrigued me. In the redwoods of Northern California, the location seemed perfect, far enough away from everything but close to mountains and a day's drive, at most, to the coast.

It had taken less time to get my retirement pushed through than I had expected. Manning had coordinated our meeting to coincide with when I needed to either renew my contract or part ways.

Manning forwarded my case up the ladder, and someone called in a favor. Next thing I knew, I was out of a job. I did hit the beach at first, ignoring the estate. I took a page out of Gardner's playbook, drank a bit too much and fraternized with the opposite sex.

That lasted almost two whole weeks. I was too bored sitting around on my ass, doing nothing. So, I picked a property at random, and now I stood in the middle of this semi-neglected house with a tape measure in one hand and a growing shopping list for the hardware store in the other.

The house had what designers called 'good bones'. It was well-built and had belonged to my great-grandfather, and for a time, my grandfather before he moved the family back east. That's where my father had been raised. Where I had been raised. But there was something about this house that spoke to me. Maybe that's what Manning had said about finding my soul? I had roots here that I barely understood.

And this part of California. The trees were majestic, the sky crystal clear. And while it was cold enough for snow, it didn't seem to be that same bone-deep cold that never went away that I had remembered as a kid in Chicago.

Well, if I were ever going to get anything done in this place, I was going to need a few supplies. I didn't trust the ancient brooms and mops I had found to do much more than spread dirt and dust around.

I needed an industrial shop vacuum, dust rags, brooms, garbage bags, all of it.

Flat Rock wasn't a big town, but it was big enough to have the essentials. I drove into town and out the other side to where the big grocery store was located. I filled my shopping cart with brooms and paper towels and garbage bags, checking each item off my list after I added it to my collection. Since I was there, I grabbed some beer and the few things I would need to make sandwiches.

I stared at a jar of mayonnaise and contemplated my electrical situation. Was I willing to waste money on what would most likely be a single-use purchase? Did I trust the old refrigerator enough to risk food poisoning by using the mayonnaise again tomorrow after opening it today?

I took my pen and wrote *New Fridge* on the shopping list.

For anything that I couldn't buy in town, including a new refrigerator, I could head down the road for an hour and find what I needed in Redding. Or I could just order something online and have it delivered. Of course, I needed to get an internet connection up at the house before I could do anything online.

I loaded the back of my truck up with my purchases. I still needed a shop vac. I looked at the bags in the truck bed and decided to head home and drop them off before getting back on the road to Redding.

I turned onto Main and headed north. In my peripheral vision, I saw a blur heading toward the street. I slammed on my breaks. The blur was a kid on a skateboard. I didn't want to hit him, but I wasn't so sure he wasn't going to hit me. The idiot headed straight into the road. He hit the curb and fell out of sight.

I slammed the car into park and was out in a flash. The kid was on the ground. He looked like a pile of old men's clothes that were too big.

"Why the hell are you skateboarding in the snow?" I yelled at the kid. I couldn't believe how stupid he was being. He could have been killed. What if I hadn't seen him?

"Because there's snow? Maybe because I thought falling in the snow would be softer. Guess what? It's not." The kid sneered back at me.

"Fuck." I saw it was a girl. "Sorry, I mean, crap, are you okay?"

"I'm on my ass, holding my arm. Do I look okay?"

I shouldn't have laughed, but the words coming out of that small, near angelic face were just wrong. She glared at me. All I could think of was *tempest in a teacup*. She was small and full of rage. And probably a lot of pain.

"Let's get you up." I leaned toward her.

Her squeal was high-pitched and full of fear. "Don't touch me, don't touch me."

I pulled my hands back and away. "Okay, okay. I won't touch you unless you give me the word. But you need to get up before you get too cold. I don't want you going into shock."

She sat there hugging her arm. Her eyes darted about. "Will you grab my skateboard?"

"Sure thing, kid. What's your name?"

"Ruby."

I jogged across the street and back, sticker covered skateboard in hand. I tossed it into the back of the truck.

She had managed to shift so she was up on one knee and about to push up onto one leg. She started to go up but wobbled and started to fall forward.

"I got you." I caught her around the waist and pulled her all the way to her feet.

"Hey, what happened to consent and not touching me?" She was not giving an inch. Good for her, she was a spitfire.

"Sorry, but you were about to go down, face first."

"Yeah," she said softly. Her voice suddenly became very small. "Thank you."

"You want to call your mom?" I asked.

She shrugged. "I don't have a cell phone. She's going to be pissed about this. You think you could give me a ride to Burger Jeff?"

"Burger Jeff?" I didn't think those were still around. "You mean the hospital. You need X-rays and to have your arm set."

"Kenzie works at the Burger Jeff. She'll take me to the clinic. I don't need my arm set." Ruby tried to sound tough, but she winced with every other word.

"Try wriggling your fingers," I told her.

She screamed. All the color in her face turned green, and she looked like she was going to pass out. Consent be damned. I scooped her up, opened the passenger door, and put her on the seat in my truck.

"Hey!" she started.

"Sit down before you fall down. I'm taking you to the hospital. You can use my phone to call your mom, or Kenzie."

Poor kid didn't even look like she had it in her to nod. She rested her head back and turned, pulling her legs inside. I closed the door and walked around to climb in on my side. I started the truck and put it into gear.

"Can you help me with the seatbelt? I can't do it." She didn't sound good. All that anger and adrenaline were abandoning her. She sounded like a scared little girl now. As I leaned toward her, she flinched away. She was scared, and I wasn't helping. I was probably grimacing and growling under my breath. I sat back into my space and tried to not look like I was barking orders at a bunch of soldiers.

"My name is Major Tate Bowers, U.S. Army, retired. I'm not going to hurt you. Let's get you buckled up so I can get you to the hospital."

She gave me the briefest of nods. I reached across her to grab the seatbelt. With some careful maneuvering so that the strap didn't go over her injured arm, I got her buckled in.

"Army, huh? No wonder you're so bossy."

I chuckled. She was starting to feel a little better.

"When we get to the hospital, I'll call your mom for you. I'll explain everything."

"Not my mom, Kenzie." There was that name again.

"We should let your mom or your dad know. You can tell your friend later."

"I don't have a mom or a dad. I have Kenzie, my sister. She's my legal guardian." Ruby sounded tired. Probably the pain catching up to her combined with my dumb ass not knowing her situation.

"Sorry, yeah. When we get there, I'll call Kenzie for you."

4

KENZIE

"Will you get me a refill, darlin'?" Mac held up his paper cup and waggled it in my direction. The ice cubes clacked about as much as ice can rattle against paper. Had that cup been glass, the noise would have been loud and pulled everyone's attention in the dining room to him.

I was a row of tables over sweeping up French fries after some kid threw them around. I swear there were more fries on the floor than that kid could have possibly eaten. "It's not that kind of restaurant, Mac. Get your own."

"But it tastes better when you do it, Kenzie," he cajoled.

I would say he was whining, but did men in their fifties whine? Ruby whined, and it had a very similar grinding feeling in my ears.

"After everything I've done for you, the least you could do is refill my Coke."

I hated it when he pulled that card. The 'I helped you, now you help me.' Sure, he stepped in when my parents died. But wasn't that what people were supposed to do? Be helpful after tragedy strikes?

I let out an exasperated sigh. "Give me a second." I lifted up my broom and dustpan to show him I needed to put my tools away.

"My tongue is gonna curl up and turn to dust by the time you get back here."

"Then get it yourself," I quipped back.

"You keep me on my toes, girl. I like that about you. But you know, you'll catch more flies with honey."

"I'm not sure what's funnier, your thinking I want to catch flies or your not realizing you just called yourself a fly. Bug is about right."

Mac laughed. I wished I had been trying to be funny. I wasn't. He was bothering me, and somehow, every time I tried to brush him off, I only ended up encouraging him more.

"Kenzie, you really do make me work for your attention. When are you going to stop being so hard on me?" Mac Campbell had been friends with my father. Somehow, I couldn't help but think if my dad were still around, Mac wouldn't talk to me this way. Or maybe he would. But if Dad had lived, I would have finished school, and I wouldn't be stuck working in fast food where Mac could come and pester me with his order of fries.

"Now, Kenzie, that's no way to—"

"Hey, Kenzie, you have a call back in my office," my manager, Will, called out.

"Sorry." I made my eyes go wide and shrugged at Mac.

I scurried back to the *Employees Only* door and pushed into the back kitchen area of the place. "Thanks for rescuing me from Mac. He won't leave me alone. Can't you do something about him?"

"He's harmless, Kenzie. He's been a friend of your family for years. If you want him to leave you alone, you'll just have to figure it out."

"If you talked to him, I wouldn't have to. But this works too. I can find something to do back here until he leaves."

Will shook his head and pointed to his office. "I didn't call you back here to get you away from Mac. You have a call. It sounds serious."

"What?" I ran into the back. Ruby knew she wasn't allowed to call me unless it was urgent and she couldn't get herself to the restaurant. It was late enough that it wouldn't be one of her teachers, not that Ruby's teachers ever needed to call me. But I couldn't think of why anyone would be calling, let alone something that would sound serious.

"Hello?" My heart pounded in my throat. The word came out on a squeak.

"Kenzie? I'm here with Ruby, hold on." the voice was deep. Was he a cop? Why was Ruby with a man?

"Ruby?" I yelled.

"Don't get mad, Kenzie," Ruby started.

Mad? I wasn't mad, I was panicked. "Where are you? What's going on?"

"I fell, and he insisted, and it's not my fault." I heard voices and then it wasn't Ruby on the phone anymore.

"Kenzie? I insisted on bringing Ruby in to the ER. She fell and broke her wrist."

"It's not broken," I heard Ruby moan in the background.

"Where are you?" I asked.

"We're at Shasta County Hospital," the man said.

I hung up the office phone and ran. I paused long enough to grab my purse and keys. "Will, Ruby is in the ER. I have to go, sorry."

"You can't just run out of here. You're on the schedule," Will started.

I paused long enough to glare at him "My little sister is in the ER with a stranger. She's all I've got." I kept my eyes locked with him, daring him to say anything, daring him to fire me.

He stared back, but his eyes dropped away before I blinked. "I'm just saying, you didn't clear this with me first."

"What part of an emergency gets scheduled in advance?" I left him with that nugget of logic.

I white-knuckled the steering wheel the entire drive to the county hospital.

"Oh, come on!" I couldn't find a parking place once I arrived.

By the time I found parking and managed to run into the ER waiting room, I was panting. My heart hadn't stopped racing since the man said he took her in. I more than half expected to see her sitting with a cop. Who else would pick a kid up off the ground and take her to get her wrist X-rayed?

Apparently, that guy. I stopped breathing for a second as I saw who Ruby was sitting next to. She looked tiny curled up on the seat, feet tucked in under her. She cradled something in her arms like a baby and was tucked in under the man's arm.

He sat with a protective arm around her, and he looked, well... so many thoughts raced through my head all at once. He looked fierce, someone whom maybe I should be afraid of, but he was stunning. And I'd seen movie stars come through town on their way to the ski slopes, and this man was even better-looking than some of them.

Hot man occupied my thoughts for a second or less. Ruby was hurt, and he was sitting there protecting her. I owed him.

"Ruby?" I skidded to my knees in front of her. I didn't care if I got my uniform dirty. The floors at the hospital were probably cleaner than anyplace else, anyway.

She lifted her head and looked at me. She looked pale.

29

"The pain started to really kick in about fifteen minutes ago," the man said.

I looked up at him then. His eyes were so kind. How had I thought he was intimidating?

"Why haven't they given her anything?" I asked.

"They won't give her anything until they take her back," he said.

I didn't like that answer. I pushed to my feet and stormed over to the triage nurse. "My sister is in a lot of pain."

"I just explained to them that we can't give her anything out here. They will determine a course of treatment once they get her back."

"How soon is that going to be? How long has she been here?"

The triage nurse looked at me like I was getting on her last nerve. "I don't know, I checked her in maybe twenty or thirty minutes ago. Look, we're busy this afternoon. Be grateful they didn't take her straight into the back. At least that way, you know she's not critical."

Not critical. Ruby's injury could wait. Part of my brain latched onto that and found comfort in it. Another part of me thought that it was Ruby. A splinter was critical. They should be treating her immediately. I slumped my way back to the seats. I sat next to Ruby. She didn't shift. She continued to lean into her rescuer and not me.

"I'm sorry, I didn't get your name. What happened?" I asked.

"Tate Bowers. Sorry we couldn't be meeting under better circumstances." He reached across Ruby and took my hand.

His hand was rough. He worked with his hands. The skin around his eyes looked like he spent a lot of time outdoors. He could have been a lumberjack, or in construction. As he continued to hold my hand, I became keenly aware that I smelled of fry grease.

"Ruby was skateboarding, and I think she hit a curb. She went down right in front of my truck. She didn't want to come in. Said you'd be mad. I've seen a break or two in my line of work. If you need to be mad at anyone, be mad at me. I insisted."

"I'm not mad." I laughed with relief. Ruby would have tried to hide an injury from me. She wouldn't have admitted that she had been hurt at all. "This is going to cost so much. Hopefully, the insurance will cover it." I wasn't really talking to anyone, just thinking out loud. I couldn't work any more shifts at the Burger Jeff, but maybe I could pick up more work from Sally's Bridal. I could always get a third job.

I covered my face with my hands and tried to disappear for a moment. I didn't want to deal with any of this right now, not the future hospital bills, not Ruby being hurt, and definitely not the hot man who was still hanging out with us.

"Um, Tate, I'm sorry. We have taken up so much of your time. You don't need to wait around here any longer. I'm sure you were in the middle of doing stuff when you brought Ruby in."

He shook his head. "I think I'd like to stick around until I know they've taken her back there to be treated, if you don't mind. I always stay with a fallen soldier until I know they are in good hands."

Soldier? "Are you in the Army?"

"Recently retired."

5

TATE

At some point, Ruby stopped running her mouth. She pulled in on herself, becoming a smaller and smaller ball. By the time she was tucked up against my side, I couldn't resist the urge to put my arm around her. How hurt was this child that she sought comfort from a stranger?

There was more to her story than some flippant attitude and a broken wrist. I don't think she was aware that she let out soft, audible whimpers.

"Ruby?"

Instinctually, I braced, protecting my own. Ruby wasn't one of my men, but in the few minutes of her succumbing to her pain, she became mine to protect. A left-over hazard of the job. However, it didn't look like I needed to protect her from Kenzie. And I had to assume the beautiful woman rushing toward us was her older sister. There was a similarity to their features. They were clearly related.

I cleared my throat and reminded myself to focus on the situation, not the curves under Kenzie's fast food worker's uniform. Never thought polyester work pants and a corporate Polo could be so attractive on a body. Then again, Kenzie had one hell of a body.

Distractions aside, I managed to fill Kenzie in on our current status. I admired her gumption, and her ass when she got up to ask the triage nurse why Ruby wasn't being taken into the back. She returned to sit with us before I managed to finally introduce myself. Her hand was so small and soft in mine, I didn't want to let her go. Something stirred in my chest. Something bigger and stronger than the protective urges I already had for the little sister. I could already tell they were going to end up being important to me. Maybe that was just wishful thinking as I looked at Kenzie. Or maybe I wasn't really thinking. My blood supply was leaving my brain for regions south of my belt.

"Retired Army, okay. Really?" she asked.

The uncertainty in her voice caught me off guard. Then again, it was safe to say that so far, both of these sisters had me off balance in one way or another.

"What? You sound dubious."

"Nothing, I just thought you looked like an expensive lumberjack, but the Army makes more sense."

I ran my hand over my jaw. I had a few days' worth of stubble, but nothing that could be called a beard. "I don't have enough facial hair to be a lumberjack," I complained.

"Excuse me, are you Ruby's guardian?" The woman wasn't dressed like a nurse, but she had the same style of ID badge clipped to her collar.

"I am," Kenzie answered.

"I need her insurance card. Can you come with me, and we can get her checked into the system?"

Kenzie gave me a wry grin as she stood and followed. She came back a few minutes later and sat with a heavy sigh.

Ruby whimpered. I gently patted her back and made a soothing sound at the same time Kenzie did. Our hands brushed. I was very aware that was not the moment to feel something for Kenzie, but there was a buzz of something more than static electricity when we touched. She glanced up at me, and our eyes locked. Her large, luminescent eyes were the sacred pools of a siren, luring me into their depths. I don't know how long we stared into each other's eyes like that. The connection that was happening between us was shattered moments later.

"Ruby," a nurse with a clipboard called out.

"Hey, kiddo, you think you can walk?" I leaned over to look at the kid under my arm when she didn't immediately jump up as I expected her to.

Kenzie was on her feet and was coaxing Ruby to move.

She moaned and shifted.

"Are you kidding me? You are not asleep," she scolded.

"No, but moving hurts," Ruby moaned.

She had been full of sass and sarcasm, but now she just sounded like a wounded little girl.

"Thank Mr. Bowers for bringing you to the ER and calling me," Kenzie directed.

Ruby moved slowly, as if everything hurt. She didn't look like she could focus very well when she looked at me. She managed to nod. Her skin looked almost green around the edges of her mouth and under her eyes. I had seen that look of pain before. The body was barely managing to hold it together.

She took one step away, Kenzie started to say something, and for a second time that day, I was catching Ruby as she started to go down.

"Ruby? Ruby!" Kenzie started yelling.

Clipboard nurse was suddenly next to us, no longer waiting impatiently by the double doors.

"I've got her," I said.

"Can you carry her, or should I get a chair?" the nurse asked.

"Lead the way."

"Are you sure you can carry her? She's not as small as she used to be." Kenzie started to hover around like a frantic bee.

"She's a lot lighter than some of the men I've had to carry. I'm good."

"Wha—?" Ruby started to smack her lips like her mouth was dry and sticky.

"It's okay, Ruby, you passed out. Can we get her something for the pain?" Kenzie asked as we followed the nurse down the hall and finally into a room.

I set Ruby onto the bed. "There you go. They'll take good care of you."

"I can't thank you enough, Mr. Bowers, for being in the right place at the right time," Kenzie started.

"Tate. Mr. Bowers was my father. I'm glad I could help out." I put my hand on Ruby's leg. "You take care, okay?"

"Don't go," Ruby whimpered.

"Ruby, we need to let... Tate get on with his day."

I smiled at her hesitation at saying my name. I liked the way my name sounded on her lips. I liked the way her name felt in my mouth. I was thinking way too much about her lips and kissing her when I should have been more worried about Ruby. Maybe I was allowing myself to be distracted because Ruby was safe?

I shook the thought off. I had spent far too many years being on constant alert. This distraction in the form of Kenzie was almost worrisome. Almost. She was a lovely distraction, and I wouldn't mind discovering just how distracting she could be.

"I can stick around for a little bit," I said with a shrug. Any excuse to stay and get to know Kenzie. "How about this? I'll stay until they take you back for X-rays."

I knew they would get her wheeled off to the X-ray room sooner rather than later. I wanted to stick around, but I also didn't want to seem like some kind of creep, overstaying my welcome. I stood out of the way, my hands shoved into my pockets. Kenzie sat nervously on the one chair in the room.

A different nurse swept into the room.

"Can my sister have something for the pain?" Kenzie asked. She sounded desperate.

I wanted to reach out and touch her, offer support and comfort. But I was a stranger, and she hadn't sought refuge with me the way Ruby had.

"Sorry, not until the doctor reviews the X-rays in case they have to do a surgical reset."

"Oh, crap, that's going to be so expensive," Kenzie said under her breath. I know I wasn't meant to hear that.

"What happened? Skiing?"

"Fell off my skateboard," Ruby groaned.

"Were you wearing a helmet?"

"Always," Kenzie growled. "You were wearing your helmet, right?"

"Yes, I was wearing my helmet." From Ruby's annoyed response, I figured this had been a much-discussed situation.

"Did you hit your head? Can we see the helmet to make sure?" the nurse asked.

"I don't know," Ruby said.

"Where is your helmet?"

"Oh, right, it's in Tate's car with my board," Ruby said.

"I'll be right back," I announced as I pushed off the wall. I jogged outside and grabbed Ruby's helmet and board from the back of the truck and headed back inside.

"Where do you think you're going?" The triage nurse stopped me as I headed toward the double doors that led into the area with the ER rooms.

I held up the helmet and board. "I need to give these back to Ruby."

"Ruby?"

"The kid I brought in with a broken wrist," I clarified.

"Yes, What's her name?"

"Ruby," I repeated.

"Her full name?"

I looked at the woman and tried really hard not to glare and to not shift into officer mode. I couldn't pull rank on her. She wasn't a soldier, and I wasn't in the Army any longer. With a grimace, I shook my head. "Not a clue," I admitted.

"Well, family members only," she said rather smugly.

"I've already been back to the room with her. I carried her back there," I tried to explain.

"I'm sorry, but rules are rules. We have to protect our patients."

She had a point. I didn't have to like it, but I would abide by her rules.

I held out the items. "Would you please make sure that Ruby gets these back?"

She took the helmet, glancing at the collection of stickers, and sneered as she took the board. "I will, thank you."

I turned to leave, and then a thought hit me. I strode up to the window where Kenzie had checked in.

"Look, I know you can't tell me patient names, but can you tell me how much this is going to cost? Does she have a copay?" I explained exactly what I wanted to do.

The woman took my credit card with a smile. "This is the nicest thing I think I've ever seen anyone do."

6

KENZIE

"I'll be right back." Tate gave me a nod as he left.

"You should date him," Ruby mumbled.

"Ruby!"

I couldn't believe she said that with the nurse standing right there. Before I had a chance to say anything, there was a flurry of activity and commotion at the door to the little room we were in.

"Ruby Hart?" Yet another nurse, or maybe this was an orderly, came in with a wheelchair.

"That's me."

"I'm here to take you to get X-rays."

I got up and shuffled out of the way. The room was getting crowded, and I kept looking for Tate to come back. With the orderly's help, Ruby climbed out of the bed and sat in the chair.

"Do you need me to come with you?" I asked.

"Tate said he'd come back with my stuff," Ruby said.

"You can wait here," the nurse said at the same time that Ruby spoke.

I nodded. Right, Tate was coming back with Ruby's helmet and skateboard. As if I had forgotten. I hadn't. I was very aware that Tate said he was coming back. Not only was he insanely handsome, but he was also strong. He carried Ruby as if she weighed nothing. Maybe for someone built like him, she was easy to lift. To me she was like a cinder block. There was no way I could pick her up.

The nurse stayed and arranged something before giving me an awkward smile and then leaving. And then I was all by myself, waiting for Tate and Ruby to both come back. He should have been back by now. How far away was his truck?

I sat there and played with my fingers. I was too distracted to read the romance novel I had in my purse. I didn't have one of those smart phones with video games. We kept a small prepaid cell phone at the apartment for emergencies, but other than that, Ruby knew the phone number for the Burger Jeff, and I memorized all of her friends' phone numbers.

I wished Tate would come back. He would distract me from the anxiety building in my middle. My worry bounced back and forth between how badly Ruby was hurt, how much this was going to cost, and what was taking him so long? I got up and stuck my head out the door. The hallway was empty. I didn't want to go looking for him in case Ruby came back.

"Can I help you?" another nurse asked.

"I was just looking for the gentleman who was with us. He left to get something from his truck. I thought he said he would be right back."

"You can go look to see if he's in the lobby." She pointed over her shoulder.

"Yeah, I don't want to leave in case my sister comes back and the doctor comes in while I'm gone," I admitted.

"The doctor won't talk about a treatment plan without you there. You have time to run out and see if your friend is still here."

I said a quick thanks and scurried to the lobby. I must have been more nervous than I had realized because when I didn't see Tate sitting in the lobby, I felt disappointment roll over me. I wasn't fair. He had just left without saying goodbye, without giving Ruby her skateboard back. My disappointment quickly turned into resentment and annoyance once I realized he hadn't brought her stuff back. So much for being one of the good guys. He had stolen a kid's skateboard. Who did that?

"Screw him," I bit out under my breath.

With a huff, I turned to go back into the back and wait for Ruby.

"Miss Hart?"

"Yeah?" I turned to see the very first nurse I had spoken with when I had arrived approaching me. She held out Ruby's belongings.

"That man left these for you. They're yours, right? I got the right person?"

"My sister's. Thanks. He didn't say anything, did he?" I asked. What was he going to say? He realized he had a life that didn't involve scraping skateboarders off the pavement and waiting around in hospital ER rooms with people who smell like stale French fries? No, he didn't need to say anything, but a goodbye would have been nice.

Tucking the skateboard under my arm, I took the helmet and retreated back to Ruby's room. I pulled on my collar and sniffed my shirt. I reeked of the kitchen at work. I should apologize to each and every nurse for stinking up the place.

Ruby was back in her room when I got there. We didn't wait long before the doctor came in with a tablet and showed us the images of her wrist. She got lucky. It wasn't so bad that she would need surgery, but she wasn't going to enjoy the resetting process. They gave her a

41

light sedative, but that didn't stop her from yelling or from crying. And it didn't stop me from crying for her. Fortunately, it didn't take very long, and then Ruby was picking out a purple wrap for her cast.

"You're all set. The nurse will give you follow-up care instructions." The doctor stood. The accompanying nurse cleared away the scissors and the cast materials. "Keep wearing that helmet."

He patted Ruby on the opposite shoulder and left.

I watched the nurse, anticipating her to say something, but she just smiled and told us to take care.

"Can we leave yet?" Ruby sounded exhausted. I didn't blame her one bit. She was probably still a little wobbly from the sedative.

"As soon as they say we can." It felt like another hour, but it was probably less than ten minutes before one of the first nurses we saw came in with a printout of instructions. "Do you have any questions?"

I read over everything before I let her leave. I had to know what kind of pain medicine Ruby could take and whom to call to make a follow-up appointment with.

"Thanks, I think we're good," I said once I had my answers.

As soon as she left, Ruby scrambled to get her things. She looked at the helmet in her hands and the skateboard I was holding out to her. She thought about it for a minute before putting the helmet on her head like a hat and taking the board with her good hand. She led the way back out through the ER waiting room.

"Hold on a second. I need to check on something," I told Ruby.

She huffed and rolled her eyes. She was as ready to be out of this place as I was. She took a seat in the waiting room.

"Excuse me," I said to the lady who had taken my insurance information. "Do you know if the hospital will let me make payments? Or if I can apply for one of those medical credit cards?"

"Yes, we can make payment arrangements." She opened a drawer and rummaged around before handing me a folded brochure. "Here's the information if you want to get a Care Credit account. They are very helpful, no interest if you pay it off in a year. But I think your bill has already been taken care of."

"What?" I couldn't have heard her right.

She focused her attention on the computer at her desk, fingers pecking away at the keyboard. "Yep, Hart, Ruby, paid in full."

I shook my head. I didn't understand. "How?"

She gave me a little shrug. It looked like she was happy to be able to give me such good news, and it was good news. It was fantastic news.

"It looks like someone has anonymously paid your anticipated fees."

I deflated. Anticipated. There were always extra fees, always. I'd still owe a chunk of change. "So, I'll get a bill after my insurance pays?"

She shook her head. "No, this says paid in full. So whoever must have paid extra."

"Who would have done that?" I didn't know anybody with that kind of money. There were plenty of rich people in town. I just didn't know any of them.

"I don't know, it says anonymous."

How was I supposed to thank someone I didn't know? "Thanks."

I left her window in total shock. Laughter bubbled up the more I wrapped my thoughts around the entire idea. Someone had covered Ruby's expenses.

"What are you so happy about?" Ruby grumbled at me as I walked back to her.

"They just told me that your hospital bill has been covered," I told her.

"Huh?"

"Someone paid off your hospital bill."

"I thought that's what insurance was for. You're always freaking out about making sure you work enough hours to qualify for it."

It looked like I was going to have to sit down and have another 'this is how life works' chats with my sister. Every time she didn't understand how something worked, that I'd had to learn the hardest way possible, I made sure to tell her. She might not remember, and she might think I was boring, but I didn't want navigating the grown-up world to be as big of a shock for her as it was for me.

"Insurance only pays for part of it, then there are these things called a deductible and out of pocket expenses. And we have to pay that part. After we meet the deductible, the insurance will pay even more. I'll explain later," I said. I was tired.

"Do you think Tate could have paid it?" Ruby asked. "He drives a really nice truck."

"I doubt it. I mean, he didn't even bring your helmet and board back, just handed them off to the nurse. He did a very nice thing by bringing you in and making sure you got taken care of. But I doubt he would have paid off a hospital bill. That's a lot of money."

Anything over a hundred dollars was a lot of money in my fiscal vocabulary. Maybe he could afford a larger bill, but I doubted it.

"If you found out he paid it, would you date him?" Ruby teased.

I smacked the back of her helmet, conveniently perched on her head. "Stop it. You know I don't date."

If I found out Tate Bowers had paid Ruby's hospital bill, I'd kiss him.

7

TATE

I t was the suffocating darkness that did it. The flashes, the bangs, the light, the sound, and the sickening stench of blood and bowels could weave in and out through my dreams, and somehow, none of that bothered me. At least not on a level I was aware of. But when the action in the dream stopped, that's when I stopped being able to identify anything as a dream. I could no longer separate myself from what was happening. Because my dreams were like watching the worst possible movies with surround sound and a complete sensory experience.

But the darkness, the small space getting smaller. The pine box being lowered into the ground. The patter-patter-patter of dirt being tossed on top of the box, that was happening to me. I couldn't move my arms to try to claw my way out. I couldn't catch my breath to scream.

I woke up with a jolt. Sweat covered my body. I tossed my arms around and sucked in air. My room was too dark. I launched out of bed, hitting the light switch on the far wall. I paced back and forth a few times, trying to get my pulse to settle.

This wasn't going to work. I grabbed my robe and headed downstairs. I needed a distraction, I needed lungsful of cool air under a wide-open sky.

"Fuck." The air was colder than I anticipated as I stepped out onto the back stoop. The socks on my feet were not thick enough to keep my toes warm. I didn't care, I needed to get out from under the ceiling. The sky opened above me, blanketed with stars. I let out a heavy breath. I was not being shipped home in a pine box.

I stood out there, staring into the night sky until I couldn't handle the cold. I didn't exactly want to go inside, but I would get frostbite if I stayed out in just my pajamas and robe. I already couldn't feel my toes.

Turning on every light as I made my way through the house, I blessed my great-grandfather for high ceilings. Calvin's baseball sat on the table next to my laptop. There were some days it wasn't out of my sight, and others, I barely remembered its existence. It was going to be with me all day today.

I gripped it firmly in my hand and climbed the stairs. I might as well get dressed. It wasn't like I'd be able to close my eyes again tonight.

After countless hours of hauling and sorting, I found myself in need of a pair of long-nosed pliers. I headed into the barn. It was full of tools. There was bound to be pliers and any tool I could think of out there. Only it was so packed in with boxes and old furniture, there was no way I would find what I needed this week.

I went back into the house to grab my coat. Without thinking, I put Calvin's ball in my pocket before grabbing my keys. A short drive later, I parked in front of the hardware store. I had a mental list to pick up a few essential tools—a hammer, a wrench set, screwdrivers, and long-nosed pliers.

As I got out of the truck, I saw Ruby glide toward me, her posture on the board relaxed even with an oversized backpack hanging behind her.

"Your sister let you back on your skateboard?" I called out.

She stepped off the board with a few jogging steps before stepping on the back end of the board, popping its wheels off the ground. She caught it with ease.

She was a better skater than I had realized when I saw her lose control and fall a few days earlier.

"Like she could stop me."

"You're really good at that, aren't you?" I asked. "Are you feeling better?"

"Oh, so you're being all nice now?" Ruby was as transparent as a window, and she was angry with me.

"What did I do?" I only took her to the ER and stuck around until her sexy sister showed up and then didn't leave when I probably should have because I wanted to stick around and have Kenzie smile at me again. And I didn't come back with her skateboard.

"Are you mad at me because I had to leave your skateboard with the nurse?" I asked.

"You said you'd come back, and you didn't." Her lower lip protruded in a pout.

I leaned back and crossed my arms. "That first nurse wouldn't let me back in to see you. She said family only."

"You could have told her you were my dad."

I chuckled. I was certainly old enough to be her father. Some days, I didn't feel that old. The other day, being around Ruby and Kenzie, I certainly hadn't felt my age. And then there were days like today where I felt every day of my age and then some.

I shook my head. "She already knew we weren't related."

"Well, you could have waited for us in the waiting room," she said.

47

"You're right, I could have. But that hadn't occurred to me. I'm sorry I disappointed you. I like the color you picked," I said, nodding toward her cast.

She lifted her arm and glanced at it. "It's all bumpy. I can't put stickers on it, they just fall off."

"Stickers? Is that what kids do with their casts these days?"

She twisted up her face. Clearly, I was speaking in 'old person' terms.

"I don't know. It's what I wanted to do. Tell me something, will ya?"

I nodded.

"How come all the older grown-ups keep asking why no one signed my cast? What's up with that?"

I let out a laugh. I pitched my voice up an octave or two and made it sound crackly and warbled. In my best little old man imitation, I said, "Back when I was a kid, or before that even, casts used to be plaster and a lot smoother. Kids would draw on them or sign their names. It was a way to signify well wishes, speedy recovery. That kind of thing."

"So that's why the lunch lady asked if my friends were mad at me and no one signed my cast."

I nodded. "Exactly. People get an idea in their heads about how casts are supposed to be, and unless they've had one or are a doctor, they really aren't going to know about advances in medical science when it comes to setting bones and holding them in place."

"Were you a doctor? I mean, in the Army?"

"Not me. That might have been a better use of my time." No, I spent my time making sure my soldiers made it through dangerous situations, and when they didn't… I reached into the pocket of my coat and wrapped my hand around the baseball and squeezed.

Ruby looked at me expectantly. She was a curious kid, but she didn't need to know about my gruesome past.

"I should apologize to Kenzie for not coming back. Was your sister mad at me too?"

"That's for me to know and you to find out," she said in a singsong, teasing tone.

"I'll tell her you said that when I see her." I chuckled.

"As if you could find her," Ruby retorted.

She had a point. It was a coincidence that I had encountered her in the same basic place around the same time in the afternoon. To find Kenzie, I would have to...

Kenzie had smelled like fries. I would simply have to go into every fast-food joint in a twenty-mile radius. But no, I wouldn't need to do that much work. I just needed to go to the one where the employees still wore black and gold uniforms instead of the corporate branded T-shirts that seemed to be the trend. She had been wearing a gold-zippered Polo shirt with a floppy chef hat logo over the left breast, and this town had a Burger Jeff. I had thought those had long gone out of business, and maybe they had on a national chain level. But there was still one in Flat Rock.

"I found you. I found you twice, as a matter of fact," I pointed out with a smirk.

"Well, that's because you keep driving into town at the same time I'm getting out of school."

I twisted around trying to orient myself. The school was southeast of the downtown area. She was headed toward the opposite side of town.

"You go to the library after school?"

"Yeah, so?"

"That explains why we meet again," I answered. I waved my hand around with a flourish.

"Whatever." She dropped her board back onto the street. It bounced with the pressure of her foot. "I've got homework to do before Kenzie gets home or I'll get in trouble. I have to make up for missing yesterday." She held up her cast. "It hurt too much, but she made me go to school today. So unless you're willing to give me a ride to the library, I gotta go."

I cocked my head toward the front of the truck. "Get in."

I helped her with the seatbelt. The library was less than ten minutes away. She probably would have made it in less time than it took me to drive.

"Thanks for the ride," she said as she unfastened her buckle and jumped out of the truck.

"I'll let Kenzie know you're being studious when I see her."

"You aren't going to con me into telling you where she works." Ruby leaned back into the truck and raised her eyebrows at me.

"You don't have to. I already know." I mimicked her expression.

"What? How?"

"That's for me to know and you to find out," I said back with the same inflection she had said it to me with earlier.

She slammed the door with a huff. I watched her stomp into the front of the library before I pulled away from the curb. I liked that kid. She had spunk.

8

KENZIE

Every time I shifted to work in another part of the restaurant, Mac was there. He was like a virus or a bad smell, or something that just wouldn't go away.

"Will," I called out as I pushed my way into the kitchen area. At least Mac couldn't follow me back there. Employees only.

Will quickly shuffled papers around on his desk and sat up straighter and started staring at his computer monitor intently as I walked in. He was doing important work. Sure, important. It looked like he had been playing video games on his phone to me and was now pretending to do the scheduling. I've done the scheduling before. It really wasn't that hard.

"Mac is pestering me again. Can I please do the drive-thru window? Or put me on the grill," I pleaded. Anything to get me out of the front of the place where Mac could see me, could talk to me. I had thought about getting a restraining order, but then guilt kicked in. Mac had been supportive and helpful after the crash. He covered the costs of the utility bills and showed me how to pay the rent on the house. Of course, I had to pay him back as soon as the insurance money had come in. But the point was, he had been there during the darkest part of my life to help. I couldn't just make him go away. Or could I?

I certainly had tried to set boundaries. He wasn't allowed to stop by the apartment whenever he wanted, and he was no longer allowed to pick Ruby up after school and give her rides home. At least I had asked him to stop doing that. I knew it still happened, but that didn't mean I liked it.

But work was a public location, and unless my manager, Will, stepped up and said something to Mac, there was nothing I could do.

I felt trapped, like a mouse in a maze, and Mac was a hungry cat watching my every move, blocking all the exits.

"I don't need you on the grill. I need you to make sure everything is clean."

"Swap me and Latisha. She can clean. Let me do the drive-thru."

"Latisha twisted her ankle. She can't move around a lot. The drive-thru is the only way I can keep her on the schedule," Will explained.

"Send her home. If she hurt her ankle, she shouldn't be standing at all."

Will shook his head. "She wants the hours. Tell the old guy to just order something or leave."

I let out a choppy breath, like a fake cry. "That's the problem, he keeps ordering stuff to stay."

Will looked entirely too excited by that. "Good, more sales. Tell him to go away until tomorrow."

"He won't listen to me. You come out and tell him to go away."

Will puffed up his cheeks and rolled his eyes. It was a normal expression on a teenager. It just looked ridiculous with his mustache and aviator glasses frames.

"Handle it, Kenzie. You have to learn to fight your own battles."

It was my turn to roll my eyes. I turned and left Will's office. Fine, he could sit in there and play video games, so I could avoid going out front. I leaned against the tile wall across from the drive-thru nook.

Latisha looked over her shoulder at me but didn't skip a beat when it came to taking the order.

"That will be fifteen ninety-three, pull up to the first window." She pulled the headset off her ear, wrapped her hand over the microphone, and turned back to me. "What's up?"

"How's your ankle?" I asked.

"Throbbing. Let me guess, you're staring longingly at my station because that old creep is out there again."

I nodded.

"Welcome to Burger Jeff, go ahead with your order," she said into the microphone. "No, I'm sorry we don't have Happy Meals. That's McDonalds."

She worked smoothly, taking money from the car at her window and taking the order from the car at the menu. And she still managed to have a conversation with me. She was a pro when it came to running the drive-thru. Better at it than I was. But I desperately needed to get away from Mac.

"Go clean the bathrooms. He can't follow you in there."

"He'd try, saying he needed to piss while I was in the men's room," I complained.

"That's easy. If he goes in and says he needs to use it, spill water all over the floor. Tell him to watch his step, and then you leave. And go hide in the women's restroom until he leaves. If he follows you back out, tell him you can't be in the restroom cleaning at the same time a customer is using the facilities. But spilling the water is key because he can't deny that you need to clean that up." She laid out a perfect plan.

"How did you figure all of that out?" I asked.

"I had an overbearing boyfriend, and one of my coworkers at the last fast-food place I worked at told me that little trick. Men can't go into the women's room, and they can't be in the men's room while a female employee is cleaning. If they insist, spilled mop water tends to keep anyone out of an area."

"Kenzie! Leave Latisha alone and get back to your assigned task," Will growled as he stepped out of his office and saw me loitering.

I pushed off the wall and walked toward the front area.

"Remember to put up the wet floor signs," Latisha called out after me.

I went straight to the mop closet. I liked her idea and had a plan to hide out in the bathrooms. If I did a thorough cleaning, top to bottom, that could buy me thirty minutes of time without Mac pestering me.

I pushed the bright yellow cart through the Employees Only door. I swear, Mac had to have been waiting at the closest table. He was right there next to me immediately.

"I was beginning to think you're trying to avoid me." He chuckled, like it was a joke.

"I am." I didn't smile, I didn't even look at him. "I have to clean the bathrooms. Excuse me."

I knocked on the men's room door and pushed it open. "Anyone in here?"

When I got no answer, I pushed the door open with my back and dragged the cart in after me. Mac was right there, trying to follow the cart in.

I stopped, completely blocking the door. "Do you need to use the facilities?"

"I'm trying to talk to you, Kenzie."

"And I have to work. You can't come in here while I'm cleaning. If you need to use it, let me step out."

"Why are you being so difficult today?" Mac asked.

"Mac, I have to clean the bathrooms. It's not something I want to do, and I would like to get it over with."

"Fine." He backed away.

It was a minor victory, and I knew that as soon as I was done, I would have to face him again. I set up the *Restroom Closed for Cleaning* sign and the yellow wet floor hazard A-frame in front of the door.

I always cleaned the men's room first. It was the grossest of the two restrooms, and I wanted to get it done. It was an internal tug-of-war between my need to avoid Mac and my need to get the work done and get out of the restroom as soon as possible.

Avoiding Mac won, and I did a thorough job, even washing down the walls behind the urinals. Men were so gross. Mac was still waiting for me when I transferred the cart into the other restroom. After cleaning the women's room, I took my uniform shirt off and scrubbed my face, neck, and arms. I needed to be cleaned after all that yucky work.

After putting my shirt back on, I folded all of the cleaning hazard signs up and slotted them away into their spaces on the mop cart. I pushed the cart back into the wet closet and poured the dirty mop bucket water down the drain. I did everything deliberately, meticulously, and took my time. I wasn't in a rush to get back out to where Mac had access to me again.

I couldn't avoid cleaning the tables anymore. I grabbed the spray bottle of disinfectant cleaner and a wipe cloth. Too bad I couldn't spritz Mac with the cleaning fluid.

"Now, Kenzie, I'm not going to take no from you again. I've got something to say, and you're going to listen," he said as I stepped into the front of the restaurant.

"You can talk, but I have to work. I'll get into trouble if Will comes out here and sees me chatting away with you. You get me into enough trouble as it is." Maybe if he thought I got in trouble with my boss, he would leave me alone. I had tried it before, but it never seemed to make a difference.

I tried to ignore him as I climbed into the first empty booth and began spraying down the plastic seats and table.

"This would be easier if you would look at me," Mac hemmed and hawed. Why wouldn't he just say what he needed to say and be done with it?

"I can hear you and wipe down a table at the same time."

"I've been thinking, we need to stop playing around. I want you to be my Valentine this year. I know—"

"She can't be your Valentine. She's already agreed to be mine," a deep, familiar voice said from behind me.

The hairs on the back of my neck shivered as tingles danced up and down my spine. I dropped the spray bottle. Tate was here.

I couldn't believe my ears. And when I turned around, I could barely believe my eyes. The other day, he had simply walked away without saying goodbye. I hadn't told him where I worked. But he was here.

"You need to back off there, mister. This is none of your business." Mac had lowered his voice and was trying to sound like an angry bear.

"Tate!" I launched out of the booth and hugged him. It might have been an overreaction, but I was so happy to see him.

9

TATE

Kenzie pressed her curves against me in a fierce hug. If I had known I would get this kind of a welcome, I would have come looking for her earlier. I should have come looking for her. I wobbled a bit before setting my drink and sack with my order down so I could wrap my arms around her.

I wanted to place a kiss on the top of her head. It felt like the natural thing to do. Instead, I inhaled her scent. She smelled like hamburgers and French fries. But she felt amazing.

"I'm sorry about the other day. The nurse wouldn't let me in the back. Said family only." I wanted her to know I wasn't some dickhead who'd abandoned her and Ruby.

"Who the hell is this guy?" the old guy who had been pestering Kenzie asked.

"He's Tate, and he's my hero." Kenzie kept her arms around my ribs. I wasn't complaining, not at all. But that hero comment, wow.

"You're feeding my ego," I admitted.

"I've never seen you around town before. How the hell are you her hero?"

I was going to say because I rescued Kenzie from him. I had watched her for a few moments, stunned into place with just how beautiful she really was. And this guy had been yapping at her heels the entire time.

I found the Burger Jeff easily enough. I had looked around for her at first, but I didn't see her. Maybe today was her day off? When I ordered a bacon cheeseburger, fries, and a drink, I decided to ask if she was in. What would it hurt?

"Yeah, she's around somewhere. Probably cleaning the bathrooms if you don't see her out there."

I kept scanning the restaurant. There weren't too many people around, and none of them were the pretty, curvaceous woman I would have rather dreamed of instead of reliving memories of war and death.

Just as I was about to give up, I heard her voice. I saw her round, delicious ass first, and that asshole pestering her.

But now I was her hero. Time to live up to her expectations.

"Tate carried Ruby to the emergency room when she fell off her skateboard," Kenzie said.

"If you'd listened to me, she wouldn't have that thing. It's dangerous," the old guy said. He was grumpy.

"Just a bit of bad luck," I said. "Glad I could be there to help her."

"If you let me pick her up—" Grumpy started.

"Mac, stop it," Kenzie said to him.

"I see you have time to stop and talk to him, but you won't give me any of your precious time," Grumpy, Mac, complained.

Kenzie let out a heavy breath. That sigh was something special to watch. Her plentiful breasts strained the front of her work uniform. My body remembered how those breasts felt pressed against my ribs moments earlier. My work pants started to feel tight as my body responded. She had my libido on stand-by.

Kenzie grabbed her spray bottle and started to spritz down the next booth over.

"I'm working now. Better?" she said with irritation in her voice.

Mac sat in the next booth over and twisted so he could watch her.

"Do you mind if I have a minute alone?" I asked him.

"She's working. You don't get to be alone. Besides, I was here first."

The way he said he was there first made me think he wasn't referring to that afternoon at the Burger Jeff, but in her life.

Kenzie finished the booth wipe-down and moved to another one. "Sorry, Tate. I can talk as long as it doesn't interfere with my job. You were saying the nurse wouldn't let you back, even though you had already been there with us?"

"Yeah. She was pretty adamant. I didn't want to cause a ruckus. Ruby was pretty mad at me. I wanted to make sure you weren't angry too. I should have stuck around and waited."

Kenzie put down her cloth and turned to me. "Nonsense, Tate. There was no reason for you to expect that Ruby or I wanted you to come back. I'm surprised you stuck around for as long as you did."

"Is that when she agreed to go out with you on Valentine's Day?" Grumpy Mac interjected into our conversation.

"That's none of your business, Mac." Kenzie looked at me with her eyes wide and pleading.

"Look, man, Kenzie is at work. She doesn't need either of us hanging around here pestering her. You're done with your food, and I've got mine to go. Why don't we both leave her alone?"

"Don't tell me what to do," Mac grumbled, but he got out of the booth he was in and crossed to the other side of the restaurant.

"I have a break. Meet me outside?" Kenzie asked.

I grabbed my food and headed out to my truck. My food was growing colder by the minute, not that I cared. I hadn't ordered to eat. I had ordered so that I had a reason to be in the restaurant other than to find Kenzie. I leaned against the front of my truck and waited.

It wasn't long before Kenzie ran out to meet me. She pulled a hoodie closed in front of her, protecting her against the cold.

I didn't stop the grin that crossed my face. She was a lovely woman. And when she smiled back, I felt it in my balls.

"Thanks for that, back there." She gestured over her shoulder. "I know a lot of people tell me Mac means well, but I just wish he would leave me alone."

"Does he bother you a lot? Have you told your manager?" I didn't like the thought of some guy harassing her.

She shook her head. "Will is useless. As long as Mac keeps ordering food, Will says he's a customer. Will won't kick anybody out."

"Will your manager?" I asked. Grumpy was Mac, manager was Will. I wanted to get all the names straight in my head so I could remember who needed an ass kicking and who needed a stern lecture. I was good at both.

"Look, you don't have to take me out for Valentine's Day. I don't do Valentine's Day."

"What if I want to?"

Kenzie shook her head. "I know you were doing that just to get Mac to back off."

"Not at all. I mean, sure. He was getting on my nerves, and I'm not who he was talking to. Look, Kenzie, I would very much like to take you out for dinner sometime. Valentine's Day might be a little too much pressure, but a date is a very good idea. Trust me, it's a very good idea."

She laughed. Damn, she sparkled when she laughed. She had to go out with me.

"Maybe. Give me your phone number. I'll call you."

"You'll call me? How about we trade numbers, and if I want to call you I can, and will," I said.

She shook her head. "I don't have a phone. I mean, I do, but it's strictly emergency use."

"Is that why Ruby had me call the restaurant? I thought that was because you weren't allowed to have your phone while you worked."

"No, not that Will wouldn't pitch a fit if he saw anyone with a phone out. But no phone."

"Okay, fair enough. I expect you to use this," I said as I gave her my number.

"I need to head back in," she said. She started walking backward away from the truck.

I didn't want her to leave, but she had a job. I respected that.

"Call me," I said.

Mac was waiting for her, holding the door open as she ran back inside. I didn't miss the sneer on her face when she said something to him. He stayed at the door and watched me. His expression said to me that he thought he had won. Won what? Kenzie returned to work, not to him.

I flipped him off.

That clearly pissed him off. He tossed his drink cup into the trash can with aggression as he stormed over to me. I settled back against the truck. I reached over and took a sip of my drink. This was going to be very entertaining.

Mac squared up in front of me. He was huffing and sucking wind as if the short walk over to my truck had been taxing. His face was twisted up in a snarl as he looked me up and down.

I didn't budge. The guy was inches shorter than I was, and years older. We probably weighed the same. While he carried all of his weight in his gut, I carried mine in my shoulders and legs.

His finger poked into my chest. "You," he snarled. "Stay away from Kenzie."

"I could say the same to you."

"She's been putting me off for years. I'm not going to let you come in here and sweep her off her feet. You think you're charming. Who the hell are you, anyway? Some tourist in town to ski for a week? Kenzie needs stability, somebody who is going to be around."

"And you think that's you?" I asked.

"I've lived in Flat Rock my entire life. How long have you been here?"

I didn't have an answer for him. But I didn't see how not being a local made a difference. My family had been in this town for generations, even if I hadn't.

I finally stood up to my full height. I stepped in a bit closer, forcing Mac to look up. "I will not be taking your advice into consideration. If Kenzie tells me to back off, I will. It's her call, not yours. However, if she tells me you are harassing her, then we'll be having words again."

I stepped forward again, forcing Mac to back up. And then I grabbed my food and got into my truck. Mac was still standing there glaring at me as I drove off.

10

KENZIE

My head was buzzing. It had been all afternoon. I still didn't quite comprehend that Tate had asked me out. More like demanded I go out with him. But he had done so in such an epic way that he'd also somehow managed to get Mac to leave me alone for the rest of the day.

And then there was that hug. It was just a hug, but damn, he felt good. His body was hard and strong. He didn't seem to mind that I'd squished up against him. He had wrapped his arms around me and held me. It was wonderful. Would have been more wonderful if Mac hadn't been there.

I hadn't stopped thinking about it for the rest of the day. It was a lovely daydream of what could have been if Mac hadn't been there. I could have happily chatted away with Tate as I wiped down the booths and tables. But he had a life, unlike Mac who seemed to be working full-time at annoying me. Normally, the walk home after work would clear my mind of the day's stressors, but everything swirled together in my mind this evening.

I knew what Mac wanted. He had waited a year, told me he waited out of respect for my parents before he started asking me to live with him. At first, I thought he was offering to take me and Ruby in, like adopted children. That's not what he meant, and I had been dodging his advances ever since.

I didn't want to think of Mac, not when Tate was a much more interesting prospect. He was tall and handsome, and his smile did something squirmy to my insides. And I realized I hadn't told him I couldn't date while I had to care for Ruby, an excuse I had repeated often to Mac.

I unlocked the door to the apartment. The TV was too loud. Ruby was home.

"Is your homework finished?" I called out over the noise.

She picked up the remote from where she sat on the floor. We had perfectly good furniture. Actually, we had really good furniture. Mom had good taste and they had been able to afford quality. But Ruby seemed to prefer the floor.

"All done," she answered.

"Even with the make-up work?"

"Yes." She sounded so annoyed. "I went to the library after school, did everything there."

I put my purse on the little table behind the couch and hung my coat on the hook by the door.

"If I ask you to show me…"

"Seriously? Kenzie, I did the work. It's in my backpack in my room. If you need to go look through my things, screw you. I bet Mom didn't look through your stuff!" She turned the TV up again.

She couldn't have been too mad at me. She didn't storm off into her room and shut the door.

I sat on the couch behind her.

"No, Mom didn't go through my stuff. I'm sorry. I'm trying here, Ruby. School is important. I just want you to have the best possible opportunities in life."

"I'm in the eighth grade. I don't have opportunities," Ruby mumbled.

"You do, you just don't know it yet. The study habits you form today will help you get through high school with the best grades possible."

"And I need good grades so I can get scholarships, yeah, I know." Ruby let out a long sigh.

"I don't want you to get stuck in this town like me."

She picked up the remote and turned the TV down again, but she didn't look at me.

"You mean stuck with me."

Fuck. I was saying everything all wrong. "That's not what I meant, and you know it. I meant stuck working in a fast-food restaurant with creepy old men hitting on you and not understanding that no means no, and not try harder."

"What if I like it here? What if I want to be a ski instructor and stay in Flat Rock?"

I flopped back into the cushions. "I want you to have the choice to stay if that's what you want. I want you to have the opportunities I didn't."

"What do you want, Kenzie?"

I didn't think Ruby realized just how loaded that question was. What I wanted now was so very different from what I wanted at her age or when I was nineteen.

At thirteen, Ruby was just about one year old. I wanted a little sister I could play with, one who could talk and walk and be interested in playing dress-up. I wanted a living doll. Instead, I had a baby sister who took all of Mom's attention, who was fussy and cried, and who was not potty trained. At nineteen, I wanted my parents back. I wanted to take classes at Shasta College so that I could transfer to Sacramento State and finish a degree in fashion. I didn't have big New York or LA dreams, but I did once upon a time dream about owning my own little sewing boutique. I got my sewing machine when I was fifteen. I barely used it anymore except to hem things. Now, I couldn't even get a full-time job at the local bridal shop.

"I want Mac to leave me alone."

"Really? Cause I thought you'd want to go shopping for a new dress," Ruby said.

I stared at the back of her head in confusion. She twisted around and smirked at me. She had a distinctive mischievous sparkle in her eye.

"What do you think you know that I don't?" I asked.

She practically jumped as she spun around and sat on the couch next to me. "I heard that someone in this room has a date for Valentine's Day."

"How in the hell do you know that?"

Ruby was giggling now, all animosity of our previous discussion forgotten. Flat Rock was a small town, and gossip spread fast, but there was no way that Ruby…

"Did you run into Tate today?" I asked.

"Yeah, so?"

"What did he tell you?" I was convinced that's how Ruby knew. How else would she have found out?

"Let's see. He gave me a ride to the library and said he knew where you worked. I didn't tell him, I promise. Oh, and he said the nurse kept him out at the hospital. Did he say he was sorry?"

I nodded. "Yeah, he apologized. And yes, he found me at work."

"So it's true? He came in like some kind of superhero and told Mac to fuck off?"

"Ruby, language!"

She pressed her lips shut and grimaced. "Sorry."

"You're hanging out with Jake, aren't you? He cusses too much. You know I don't want you using language like that."

"Kenzie, it's not just Jake. It's everyone. Everyone cusses." She tried to weasel out of being in trouble.

"Not everyone, not you. You're cleaning the dishes after dinner tonight. No arguments."

I pushed to my feet. I stepped into the small kitchen to see what we would be having for dinner. It looked like another chicken casserole with macaroni and cheese night.

"Sorry I dropped the F-bomb, but did that really happen?" Ruby asked, following me into the kitchen.

"Yes, Tate came in. I don't know what he said to Mac, but it seemed to work. Who told you?"

"I stopped by on my way home from the library. Latisha filled me in. She said there was practically a fight over you in the parking lot."

"Latisha is exaggerating. They didn't fight. Besides, that would be really stupid for Mac to try anything. I mean, Tate is so much bigger than him."

"He's kind of cute too. I mean, he's got that same look of all the actors you like."

"You think Tate is cute?" I asked.

"No." Ruby dragged the word out into several syllables. "You think he's hot. I'm just saying he looks like you would like him. So, are you going out with him or not?"

"Yes and no. He asked me out for Valentine's Day, but I said no, but—"

"You're going to go out with him not on Valentine's Day," Ruby finished for me.

I nodded and ran water into a pot. "What veggies do we have in the freezer?"

"California blend and broccoli," she answered.

"Pick one," I said.

I held out my hand. She placed the bag of the frozen blend with carrots, broccoli, and cauliflower into my hand. I set it on the counter next to the box of noodles and the can of chicken.

"So, if you're going out with Tate, you still need a new dress to wear."

"I can't afford new clothes right now. My checks in February are always short, so we have to be careful."

"You could use my money. My check is always the same," Ruby said.

"I appreciate the offer, but your Social Security check is for rent, not clothes I don't need."

"But you need a new dress," she practically whined at me.

I needed a lot, and a nice new dress to go out with Tate in would have been wonderful, but it wasn't in my budget.

"Why are you so obsessed with my getting a new dress?"

"That's how it works on TV, you get asked out on a date and you suddenly need a new wardrobe," Ruby said. She was right. On TV, a date was an excuse to go to the mall and have a complete wardrobe remodel.

"When a TV show starts paying for our new clothes, that's when I'll go shopping," I said. Being responsible and on a budget was boring.

11

TATE

I watched my phone like some kind of teenager. Would Kenzie call me? Why wasn't Kenzie calling me? Who didn't have a cell phone these days?

Kenzie, that's who. And that's why I spent two days staring longingly at my phone, waiting for it to ring.

Well, if I wanted to see her again, it was clear I wasn't going to get anywhere sitting around the house waiting for her. And I wanted to see her again. I tossed the baseball up into the air and caught it as I sat at the kitchen table. If I was going to go find her, I should make it look like a coincidence and not the desperate action of a horny man. She already had enough of that from the way she rolled her eyes at that grump, Mac.

I didn't want her looking at me the way she looked at him. So I needed a plan. Should I conveniently run into Ruby again at the hardware store, or just go buy fries and a Coke for an afternoon snack?

I was a grown ass man. This was ridiculous.

I set the ball down, grabbed my coat, and headed out the door. I wanted to see her. Why was that so hard to admit? I had faced down the enemies of our nation, and I was getting nervous to face down one curvaceous woman whose eyes and lips had replaced the nightmares in my dreams.

After pulling into the parking lot at the Burger Jeff, I sat in my truck. This was stupid. Maybe she didn't want to see me. Maybe I needed to take the hint that she hadn't called because she wasn't interested.

"Well, she can tell that to my face," I said as I unbuckled and climbed out of the truck.

The smells of greasy burgers and French fries assaulted my senses as I walked inside. Scanning the dining room, I didn't see Kenzie.

"Can I help you?" the young lady behind the counter asked.

I stared up at the menu board, pretending to be uncertain. I needed to stop playing games with myself, with strangers. "Yeah, large fries and a Coke. Is Kenzie around?"

"She's already left for the day." She gave me my total.

I paid and moments later, I had a paper bag with my fries and a cup full of Coke. "Do you know if she'll be in tomorrow?"

"You haven't figured her schedule out yet?"

I shrugged. "She doesn't have a phone. I don't know how else to get ahold of her."

"Well, I'll tell her you came in."

I nodded my thanks as I headed out. I made it all the way to my truck before it occurred to me that her coworker didn't know my name. How would Kenzie know who had come to see her? Did Kenzie have a lot of men coming in to find her? I knew about Mac. And now they could add me to that list.

It felt like a wasted trip. No Kenzie, no way of getting in touch with her. Grabbing a handful of fries, I shoved them into my mouth and chewed while I thought. Picking a direction at random, I drove.

Without a goal, I meandered around Flat Rock. If I were going to stay here, make this little town on the side of a mountain my home, I should at least be familiar with the area. At least, that's what I told myself as I aimlessly drove around, keeping my eyes open for Kenzie or Ruby on her skateboard. There were plenty of roads here without sidewalks and that seemed deserted. But I knew an empty country road could turn a corner and be in the middle of a neighborhood full of homes and shops.

I drove past an old, broken-down car on the side of the road. I thought the city towed that kind of thing. As I passed it, I saw someone stand up on the other side of the vehicle. There was something familiar, even though I barely caught a glimpse of them in my peripheral vision.

I scanned my rear-view mirrors. That looked like Kenzie.

I stopped the truck. The driver in the car behind me leaned heavily on their horn. I started driving again, my blinker on and looking for a place I could pull into so I could turn around.

It seemed to take forever before an opportunity to turn around presented itself. I had to turn around twice. Once to drive back to where Kenzie was broken down, and a second time to be on the same side of the road.

She looked up eagerly as I pulled my truck in behind her car. Her eyes were rimmed with pink. She brushed her cheeks. And when I stepped out of the truck, recognition put a smile on her face.

She was in my arms again, hugging me.

"Oh, my God, Tate. I can't believe it's you." There was a hitch in her voice. She had been crying.

I wrapped my arms around her back and stroked her hair. I held her for a long moment, not wanting anything to get in the way of the feeling of her pressed against me.

"What happened, Kenzie? Did you break down?"

From the age and state of her car, I think I better understood why she didn't have a cell phone. Kenzie didn't have a disposable income for anything beyond the bare minimum.

As she sniffed, she pushed out of the embrace.

I was tempted to gather her back against me, keep her safe and comfortable.

"Stupid flat tire."

"Do you have a spare? I can change it for you."

She stepped back and wiggled her key into the lock at the trunk. "I'm supposed to have one here."

The trunk popped open. Kenzie began moving a box of random items to the side. I pulled up the trunk lining. Nestled into a well in the back were a full-sized spare, a jack, and a tire iron.

I hefted the items out. Bouncing the tire on the pavement a few times to confirm it was good, I got to work.

"Thank you. You keep showing up just when I need to be rescued. You really are my hero."

I wedged the jack under the frame and began cranking it up.

"Is that why you haven't called me? You've been waiting for me to come rescue you?"

She laughed. I really did enjoy the way that sound tickled my ears. "I honestly thought you would have come by work."

"Like the rest of your suitors?" I quipped.

"Suitors? You mean stalkers. And that would only be Mac. What makes you think there are other people coming to see me? I mean, other than Ruby."

I shrugged. I pulled the tire off. "You're going to want to take this to the tire shop on the road toward Redding, see if they can patch it." I let the tire fall to the ground with a wobble. "I don't know, something the girl at the Burger Jeff said this afternoon when I asked about you."

"There's a used tire place on the other side of town. He'll be able to patch it for me," she started. "That was probably Latisha. She was messing with you."

"Is she your friend?"

"Yeah. She knows that Mac comes in and bothers me. Maybe she was trying to put you off, you know—"

"Protect you," I finished her sentence. "That's a good friend."

"She is, I think," Kenzie said.

"You think?"

"She hasn't been there very long, and I don't do much outside of work."

"You don't go out? You should be going out to the clubs, drinking and dancing. Having fun with your friends."

"I have to take care of Ruby," she pointed out.

"Ruby is old enough to take care of herself now," I said.

"Well, drinking and dancing cost money. And my budget is shot to hell this month. And now I have to get a tire fixed."

"Then you should let me take you out."

"Tate," she started.

I really liked the way she said my name. I worked through the growing lust in my body by shoving the spare tire into place and spinning the lug nuts down before tightening them.

"I'm asking, that means I pay. And unlike the assholes I keep seeing online, I don't have any expectations. You won't owe me anything."

She hesitated before continuing. I glanced up to look at her. She was blushing. The pink across her cheeks was charming.

"I told you, I don't do Valentine's Day."

"Then go out with me on the thirteenth, or the fifteenth, or later. You don't have to go out with me on Valentine's Day exactly. And we don't have to call it a Valentine's date. Are you going to make me beg?"

She giggled.

I grabbed the tire and tried to move it. It felt secure enough. I got to my feet and stretched before bending down to lower the jack. Once the car was firmly on the ground, I finished tightening the lug nuts the rest of the way. I brushed my hands together before picking the flat up and hauling it into the trunk of her car.

Kenzie picked the other tools up and put them back into their places before pulling the trunk liner back into place. She left her hands on the closed trunk and stood there for a long moment, not moving.

I wanted her to look at me. But she didn't.

"You know, Mac thinks we're dating. And Latisha told Ruby about how you swooped in and saved me from a date with him. So now Ruby thinks we're going out." She turned and leaned against the trunk, not coming close to me at all. "You know, she wanted me to go buy a new dress for our date."

I chuckled. "You don't need a new dress. Maybe something other than your work uniform, but I don't care if you show up in ratty jeans and a T-shirt." Actually, her ass in a pair of jeans would be exceptionally hot.

I held my hand out to her. She slipped hers into mine. I pulled her back against my chest. "All those people expect us to go on a date. It would be such a shame to let them down."

"It would." She tipped her face up to mine. I dipped my head to kiss her.

Somebody yelled, "Get a room!" and blared their car horn at us.

Kenzie jumped away from me as disappointment replaced the anticipation that had been building in my veins.

12

KENZIE

I only ever really got one day off a week. This wasn't it. Today, I had to run errands and do my weekly pick up and delivery at the bridal shop. I used to be able to do my weekly pick up after work at the restaurant, but apparently, someone complained about my smelling like French fries. They were worried that their dresses would smell like fry grease. It wasn't like I would take their expensive dresses inside. I always left everything safely locked in the car.

Unfortunately, the change in scheduling for the pickup and delivery cut into my precious time off. If Tate wanted to see me, he would have to adjust to my schedule. Or he could wait, like Mac, and come pester me at the Burger Jeff.

I didn't like that idea very much. And I didn't like how low on gas I was. I had dresses and a tire to deal with today. And I could use some help.

I knew I was good for a few minutes on the phone. I tracked my usage religiously. I had just renewed my minutes for February, and any unused minutes in January rolled over.

I held my breath, nervous to even use the phone for something so frivolous, and turned the phone on. I had finite minutes and limited texting.

I texted the number I memorized for Tate.

I have the day off, would you want to run errands with me? Kenzie.

His reply came almost instantly.

I thought you didn't have a cell phone?

It's for emergencies. I'll explain later. Yes or no? Here's my address. I punched in my address and hit *Send.*

On my way.

I replied with a smiley face emoji and turned the phone off. Yay, Tate was coming over to help out. I gave the living room a quick tidying up. It wasn't a complete mess, so that was good. And for once, he would get to see me when I didn't stink. I spritzed myself again with the strawberry body spray that was probably an indulgence, but I considered it a necessity.

Twenty minutes later, there was a knock on the door. I checked the peephole, and seeing Tate's broad chest filling the view, I pulled the door open.

"Hi," I said. I wasn't sure what to say next. I was so excited that he actually came over.

"I wasn't sure I had the right address," he said as he stepped in, a grin spread across his lips.

"Why's that?" I asked.

He cast his gaze around the apartment before looking at me. "Making assumptions I shouldn't be making, that's why. You didn't reply to my text."

"Sorry. I turned the phone off. I only have so much texting I can do."

"And you used some of it to text me? I'm flattered."

"You might not be when I confess to asking you to run errands with me because I wanted you to drive," I told him.

"I can drive," he said.

"Yeah, but I need you to drive. I'm low on gas, and I need to get that tire fixed."

Tate started nodding. The grin didn't leave his face. "I see. Why didn't you just ask if I could drive you around?"

I sucked in a big breath. "Tate, would you be interested in driving me around town today?"

He chuckled. "I'd love to. We can take that tire to be fixed. What else do you need?"

"I have to go to the Grocery Outlet, and Sally's Bridal too."

"The bridal store? Are you getting married?" He sounded amused.

I pointed to the pile of garment bags on the couch. "Somebody is."

"Those wedding gowns?" He crossed the living room and began lifting the edges of the bags.

There were five dresses. "Two wedding gowns, a quinceañera dress, and two winter formals," I told him. "I do overflow tailoring and hemming for Sally's. I need to drop this bunch off and see if they have anything extra for me."

"Sounds like we have a lot to get done." He scooped up the dresses and looked at me expectantly. "Shall we?"

I nodded enthusiastically and scrambled to pull my coat on and grab my purse. I opened the door for Tate. He followed me out. I locked up, and then it was my turn to follow him down the three flights to the parking lot.

"You're my hero again. It would have taken me at least two trips to get all of those dresses downstairs."

"They are an armful," he admitted. He paused next to his truck and then frowned. "Kenzie, I promise this isn't a cheap come on, and I'm not trying to be a perv. But I need you to get my keys out of my front pocket."

"You want me to stick my hand in your pocket?" I gulped.

"It's that, or you take the dresses. I can't carry these and get my keys."

And there was no way I was going to be able to hold all five dresses at once. The quinceañera dress all by itself weighed at least twenty pounds with its exaggerated full skirt of layered tulle and satin.

"Okay," I managed to say. I got up close and had to run my hand over his hip, keeping it between him and the garment bags.

"I'm not gonna lie, your hand tickles."

"Sorry," I said as I snatched it away.

"Don't be. I like you touching me. But that was the wrong side. I figured I had better say something before you accused me of setting this up."

"How could I have set this up? You picked up the dresses all by your-self." I stayed pressed in close but this time reached around from the back, not his side. I let my hand skim against his jeans, over his hip bones. I found the top of his pocket and let my fingertips dip in. He twitched a bit as I pushed my hand deeper into his pocket.

"This isn't fair. Your pockets are deep. The pockets on my jeans are a joke." I had to talk about something to distract myself, or I would be too aware that my hand was very close to his inner thigh and his manhood. I found the keys and grabbed them, pulling my hand out and away as fast as I could. The temptation to linger was too much. His keys were warm from his body heat.

I beeped the lock open on the key fob and tried not to think about what I had just done.

Tate cleared his throat. I opened the back door to the extended cab, hoping there would be a space for the dresses.

He set the dresses inside and then turned to me. He held his hand out for his keys. I set them in his open palm. He closed his fingers over my hand, capturing it in place.

"I'll need your keys to get the tire out of your trunk," he said. "Unless you have them in your pocket and you want me to find them."

He winked, and I think I might have died. My mouth went dry, and my pulse raced.

"No, no, my keys are right here," I stammered as I fished them out of my purse.

"Too bad. Climb in. I'll be right back with your tire."

My body tingled as I climbed into Tate's truck. Touching him had been amazing, awakening, more fun than I could have realized, tantalizing, teasing. It had bent my mind, and suddenly, I couldn't think of wanting to do anything more than touch him more. I wanted to press against him and feel his hard muscles against me. I wanted his arms around me. What would it be like to have him touch me?

The truck bounced a bit as he tossed the tire into the back bed.

"Ready to go? Where to first?"

"Sally's Bridal." I gave him directions.

He was the best errands buddy I could have asked for. He carried the dresses into the shop and treated them as if they were fragile. Something it was difficult to even get the owners of the dresses to do. They wouldn't break, but treating a gown that costs thousands of dollars as if it were a rugged pair of cargo pants or climbing gear always bothered me. Maybe it was because I didn't know what it was like to spend that kind of money. Some of those dresses cost more than my monthly take-home from Burger Jeff. To me, something that expensive deserved to be treated gently.

"I'll meet you back in the truck," he said after hanging the dresses on a garment rack.

"Thanks. I should be out in a minute," I replied.

"Oh, he's attractive," Connie said as she looked through the job tags, matching them up to the dresses.

"He really is," I admitted. "And super nice. Do you have anything for me today?"

"I have one dress in the back."

"Only one?" I needed more than one dress a week to be able to afford groceries. It was bad enough that I wouldn't get paid for the five dresses I'd just turned in for another week, but then to drop down to only one dress... I let out a dejected sigh.

"Only one. So, is he single?" she asked.

"Who? Tate, who just came in with me? He came in with me." I emphasized the connection a second time. There was no way I was going to let Connie try to set Tate up with one of her daughters. I was perfectly okay with her thinking he was with me.

13

TATE

Kenzie was a girl boss on a mission. She had a written list of exactly what she did and how long it took for each dress. It looked like they would be a while as she spoke with the woman at the shop. I waited for her in the truck. Her face was pinched as she carried only one garment bag back outside with her.

"They only have one dress for me this week. One." She huffed and slammed the back door after she put the dress in the truck. "I'm never going to get ahead if she only gives me one dress a week."

"How many jobs do you work?" I asked.

"Technically, only two. But I used to help Arianna sell makeup. I couldn't afford the buy-in, so she got the credit for my sales. She paid me my commission, but it was more time than it was worth."

"You sold makeup? Multi-level-marketing?"

She nodded. "I know, it only works if you can recruit people, and I was trying to sell enough to buy the kit that would let me become a recruiter, but I couldn't ever make enough sales."

"MLMs are always a scam," I said.

"But Arianna is making good money. She even has the pink car."

"She makes money by selling the recruitment kits, not the makeup," I pointed out.

Kenzie scrunched up her face. She didn't seem to like what I was saying. "I know, I had just hoped it would be my genie in the bottle, you know?"

"I do. I think we all have something we wish we could change with the press of a button…"

"Or by taking a magic pill," she finished for me. "Turn here for the Tire Guy."

She kept saying Tire Guy, and I had thought she meant a guy who worked on tires, but no, it was the name of the used tire place.

"Are you sure you want a used tire?" I asked as I turned off the truck.

"I can't afford new tires. The tires here are good. They get them from higher-end dealers. You know, little old ladies who change their tires out every year even if they don't drive. Or the crazy rich people who replace their tires if they get scuffed."

"Running on low tires is dangerous," I pointed out as I hauled the flat out of the truck bed.

"I'm very aware. But there are some things that I just have no control over. I can't exactly afford tires at any point in time, but I really cannot afford the two hundred bucks that one brand-new tire is going to cost me."

"Can I help you?" the shop manager said, walking out to meet us as we approached the front.

"I got a flat. I was hoping you could patch it," Kenzie said as I rolled the tire toward the guy.

He scooped it up, said something with a grunt, and walked away.

AVA GRAY

"And now we wait. Thanks for driving me around today. My car is on fumes, and I don't get paid for a couple more days."

"Sure, no problem. Can I ask a nosy question?"

"Depends on how nosy," Kenzie said. She gave me a once-over look as if I were about to ask what her bra size was. I didn't need to ask to know she was at least a forty-eight H. Her breasts were gloriously large. I would be able to confirm the size once I got my hands on her. Until then, my palms ached to engulf her.

"Financially nosy," I clarified.

She shrugged. "Ask. I don't hide our situation. It's not ideal, but I don't see any point in being ashamed because I don't have money."

"If you can't afford gas, what would you have done if I'd said no?"

"I'd buy gas and put off getting the tire fixed. And I'd also be able to buy more meat at the grocery store. I had to prioritize. I'm going to have to walk to and from work more this week, but having that tire is my priority. I don't want to get stuck on the side of the road without it." She paused and hummed a bit, twisting back and forth. "So, I did have a bit of a genie in a bottle moment. Someone paid Ruby's hospital bill. You wouldn't know anything about that, would you?"

The tips of her teeth pressed into her plump lower lip. She looked so expectant with her big eyes looking up at me. Damn, I could envision exactly what it would be like to look down at her with my cock in her mouth. Would she be grateful enough to suck me into that hot mouth of hers if I admitted to paying that bill?

I cleared my throat. That's not why I did it. And I wasn't going to admit it no matter how tight my balls were getting at the thought of a blow job from her mouth.

I shook my head. "Wow, that's incredible. Why would I know anything about it?"

"Worth a shot," Kenzie admitted.

"You're going to need a new tire," the mechanic said as he stepped out to us.

"I was afraid of that. You have anything for about fifty bucks?" she asked.

"I can check. It's gonna be a minute."

"I can go up to seventy-five, including tax. But I'd really like to not spend too much over sixty," Kenzie told him.

"Okay, come back this afternoon, after two. I'll have it ready for you."

Kenzie nodded and headed back to the truck.

"You're not going to wait to see if he has something in your price range?" I asked.

"He's got my price range. Now, he can look through his stock for what fits my needs. I found that if I tell him how much I can afford, he gives me a better deal."

"You budget like a pro," I said, admiring her understanding of the man she was dealing with and how she would have to adjust in other areas to accommodate for the tire.

"I budget like a person who has to know exactly what every penny is doing."

"You sound like my father." I chuckled. Only my father was juggling hundreds of thousands, if not millions, at a time, while Kenzie was managing pennies.

"Mind if we stop at the hardware store?"

"Not at all. This doesn't have to be just my errands. What are we getting at the hardware store?"

"I need an axe, for chopping wood."

She looked at me dubiously.

"I'm sure there is one tucked away in the barn, but I can't find anything. It's all crammed in so tight it might be easier to throw it all out and start from scratch."

"Starting from scratch isn't as easy as everyone seems to think it is," she said. "And I know what an axe is for."

She stared out the side window as I navigated through town to the hardware store. My purchasing an axe must seem like a luxury when I more than likely already had one.

I knew we weren't going on a date for Valentine's, but I wanted to get her something. Not chocolates, but a gift that would make her life easier.

"I haven't been here for years. I forgot it smelled like this," Kenzie said as she danced down the shopping aisle ahead of me.

"Smells like what?"

"Oil, lumber, potting soil. There's no masking the smell with lavender vanilla candles or air freshener the way other stores do."

She certainly had a refreshing perspective of things.

I picked up an axe. I hefted it, tested its weight. It wasn't too bad. It would pack a wallop. Exactly what I needed. I set it over my shoulder.

"Ready?"

"You know, you seriously look like a lumberjack."

"I think you'll change your mind once you see me chopping wood." I chuckled.

"That bad?" She giggled.

I shrugged. "I've never had to chop wood before. I have no idea whether I can."

"He can't even chop wood, but you'd rather be with him?" Mac appeared out of nowhere.

"Mac," I started. I swung the axe down to the floor.

Kenzie placed her hand in the middle of my chest. It was a small, little hand, but she commanded me with it, telling me to back down.

"Mac, I've asked you nicely to please respect my decisions. I'm not at work right now, so I can tell you to go away and leave me alone."

"He's letting you stick up for him? You don't want to be with some wimp like him. Those muscles are just for show. He doesn't know how to use them outside of a gym." Mac sneered out his words.

I growled low in my throat, but I didn't move. He wasn't going to provoke me.

Kenzie looked up at me. I took a step backward. If Mac was going to block our path, we would simply take another one.

"He even runs away from a fight."

I turned back to face down Mac. With my eyes locked on Mac, I grabbed Kenzie to me, lifting her to her toes. I stopped looking at him when I kissed her. I pressed my lips against hers and forgot everything. Kissing her had been a show of power, but the reality of my lips against hers left me completely powerless. Her lips were even softer than I had imagined. She tasted like strawberries and cream. I didn't want to set her back on her feet. I didn't want to stop kissing her at all.

"Kenzie, you're making a fool out of yourself." Mac wrapped his meaty hand around her arm, pulling her back and off balance.

She yanked her arm away. "Get away from me."

"You're making a mistake, little girl, and when you realize it, I'll still be here like I always am. I'll take you in. I know how to be patient."

"You're going to be waiting a long time," Kenzie said through clenched teeth. She grabbed my hand and pulled me from the store. The axe was left where I had set it down.

14

KENZIE

"Do you want to tell me what that was about?" Tate asked as I dragged him out of the hardware store.

"Not really," I admitted. What I wanted was for him to kiss me again. If I couldn't have that, I at least wanted to be as far away from Mac Campbell as I possibly could.

I waited next to his truck for him to unlock it.

"Am I taking you home?" he asked. His voice was so gentle, so soothing. Maybe I could tell him, maybe.

"I still need to go to the grocery store, if that's okay," I said. I didn't want to look at him. I didn't want him to see me crying.

Tate was good company and didn't push the matter. Maybe I should tell him. Mac was bound to bring it up, after all. I didn't trust him to actually leave me alone anytime soon.

"Will I see you tomorrow?" Tate asked as he pulled his truck into the apartment complex.

"I told you, I don't do Valentine's Day," I said as I grabbed all of my grocery bags and the garment bag with the dress.

"It doesn't have to be for a date, Kenzie. I like your company." He watched me load my arms up. "Are you sure you don't want any help?"

"I do this all the time. I've got it. Maybe we'll run into each other. I enjoyed this." I somehow managed to close the door with my butt. I wanted to see Tate again, but I didn't know if I would be the best company on Valentine's Day.

The next morning, I only got up to make sure Ruby had what she needed for school before I went back to bed. February fourteenth, Valentine's Day, every year for the past five years, I'd kept this day to myself. Seeing people out together being all loving hurt too much.

Grief has been described to me in different ways, a big ball in a box, or a lot of balls and a bell. Whatever the combination, the grief wound keeps getting hit either by the ball hitting the sides of the box or the little balls ringing the bell. And somehow, time is supposed to change the proportions of the balls and the bells so that the grief wound doesn't get hit as often. I could accept these theories most days of the year. But on February fourteenth, I was nothing but that grief wound being hit over and over again.

I woke up sometime in the late morning. I didn't feel any better for having slept in. It was a struggle to get up and get myself dressed. Maybe this year, I could not visit?

I flopped back into bed, thinking sleeping would be easier until I started crying again. I gasped for air as the grief grew too strong. I couldn't skip visiting their graves this year. I just couldn't.

I walked all the way to the cemetery. About halfway there, I remembered I still needed to pick up my spare tire from the Tire Guy. I'd do it on my way to work the next day. Today, I didn't want to do anything.

Ruby didn't have the same grief I did. To her, this day was more about swapping little Valentine's cards and eating heart-shaped candies. It didn't hold the same pain for her. At first, I was mad about that. I had just been mad at the world, but why didn't Ruby hurt the way I did? And then I did some growing up. Everyone faces grief differently, and a child faces it differently from an adult. Not that I would have called my nineteen-year-old self an adult. But I had been more aware of everything than Ruby had been five years ago.

I shoved my hands deeper into the pockets of my coat and wondered how much one of those puffer jackets might cost. Maybe if I started putting a few dollars away with every paycheck, I would be able to afford one next year when they went on sale? The coat I currently had, I got at the thrift store, and it really wasn't doing a very good job of keeping the cold out.

I climbed the hill on the other side of the cemetery gates. When I got to their tombstone, I brushed snow from the top of it.

"Hi, Mom. Hi, Dad," I said as I leaned on the marble stone. I couldn't hug them, so I hugged the stone that marked their final resting place. It had a heart on it. I know some people thought it was because of our name, Hart, but I selected it because my parents had been a true love story. Not even in death would they part.

I would have given anything to have them say hi back.

I stayed until threatening clouds darkened the early afternoon sky. I was too cold to feel my toes, and my fingertips hurt inside my gloves. I didn't have a car to retreat to and crank up the heat. I still had to walk home. I brushed tears from my cheeks. I didn't want to leave, didn't want to be apart from them again. But the weather was going to drive me inside if I didn't move on my own.

I would get caught out in the sleet either way. I didn't need to prolong my exposure. I sniffled my way down the hill and back alongside the road.

Cars rushed past me. It would be nice if Flat Rock could see its way to putting in sidewalks. I wasn't the only person who occasionally walked.

"Kenzie? What are you doing out here?"

I looked up to see Tate jumping out of his big red truck. I wiped at the tears that continued to run down my cheeks. So much for him not seeing me crying.

"Oh, sweetheart, what's wrong?" He bundled me into his arms and against his chest. "You're not hurt, are you? Did your car break down again?"

I shook my head. It was hard to talk when I was surrounded by his care. I fisted his jacket into my hand and let myself cry for a good, long time. He held me and let me cry against him.

After some time, I calmed my breathing, and the tears stopped. I was still blanketed in sadness, but at least I wasn't crying for a minute.

"I just came from the cemetery," I said.

"You're freezing. Get in the truck. We can talk where you can be warm."

I climbed in, surprised when Tate followed me into the passenger side. He started the truck and turned the heat on with his long arms from the passenger side. Then he held me on his lap. He coaxed me to put my head on his shoulder. He was warm and provided a solace I didn't know how to find on my own.

"I don't do Valentine's Day," I started.

Tate tensed as if to protest that this wasn't a date.

"Because it was my parents' anniversary. They loved love, and this was their most favorite day of the year. Some people love Halloween, like Ruby, and for others, Christmas is their day. But for Mom and Dad, it was Valentine's Day. I always have a hard time around their anniversary," I confessed.

Tate made a comforting humming noise and stroked my hair. He smelled nice, like clean soap and aftershave.

"I'm sorry if you thought I was pushing for a Valentine's date. I didn't know." His voice rumbled through his chest and into me. I liked the sound of his voice. Everything about him felt comforting.

"Remember yesterday when I didn't want to tell you about Mac?"

"Yeah."

"Can I tell you now?"

"Of course," he said.

"I was nineteen when my parents were killed in a car accident." I tried to keep the hard parts as clinically factual as I could. No emotion, just the facts.

"Mac was one of my dad's friends. I've known Mac pretty much my whole life. So, yeah, I totally think it's gross that he hits on me. He was there after the accident, being helpful. Being a surrogate father, or at least that's what I thought. He proposed to me for the first time almost exactly a year after the accident. As he said, respecting my grief." I shuddered at the memory.

"Your father's friend started hitting on you?" Tate stiffened under me. "Isn't he a bit too old?"

"I think so. I'm not into older guys."

Tate stiffened under my legs.

"Oh, relax, you're not that much older than me."

"I'm pushing forty," he admitted.

I stared at his face. He didn't look like he could be in his forties, but then again, I wasn't good with gauging ages.

"Forty isn't sixty," I finally said.

"Sixty? He's acting like he's a dumb teenager who doesn't understand how to talk to girls yet." Tate chuckled.

"Yeah, well I don't know whether he's dumb or manipulative. I trusted him, and in less than two years, he had managed to give me the worst advice ever when it came to the inheritance money. My parents didn't own their house. There wasn't a lot to begin with, and it's been a struggle ever since."

"Mac thinks you're going to come around and accept his proposal at some point?"

I nodded. "I've never indicated that I was interested. I'm not. But he gets very insistent this time of year."

"Do you need me to talk to him, get him to leave you alone?"

I loved that Tate was so protective. He barely knew me, yet he was willing to go up against Mac for my sake.

"No, but thank you." I tried to wiggle out of his lap and open the door.

"Where do you think you're going?"

"Home. I need to get home. Ruby has a sleepover at her friend's. I want to make sure she gets everything she needs before heading over."

"I'll give you a ride." He opened the door. I slid out onto the side of the road, and he followed me out of the truck.

"I can walk," I said.

"I know you can walk. But it's cold and getting wet out here. Get in."

I climbed back in and buckled up.

"I'm surprised you didn't ask me for a ride out here, or at least for a ride home."

"I didn't think to ask. I tend to not ask for things I can do myself."

"Because of Mac?" Tate asked.

Because people let me down more often than not. Because it never occurred to me that I could ask him to drive me around more than I already had. "Because of Mac."

15

TATE

I didn't like the idea of leaving Kenzie alone. I might have felt differently if I knew Ruby would be there to keep an eye on her. But Kenzie had said Ruby was going to be over at a friend's house. Kenzie was having a hard time. She must have loved her parents very much, and to lose them at a young age. And on top of all that grief, she had been left to have to take care of and raise Ruby.

It was a lot.

I felt bad for feeling a little jealous. My parents were gone, and I didn't notice or care. What must it be like to love someone so much that their absence caused so much grief?

I tossed my coat onto the hook at the back door as I walked into the kitchen. I saw the baseball on the table. Maybe I understood too well.

My phone buzzed in my pocket. I pulled it out, shocked to see Kenzie's name as the caller ID for the text message. Her phone minutes were a precious commodity. I was flattered she was using them to text me again.

I know I said I wanted to be alone. But I don't, she texted.

You're going to let me take you out?

No. No date. But I don't want to be alone.

You want some company? I asked.

Please. And some pizza.

I laughed. Pizza and company. Sounded like a date to me.

Tell me what you want on your pizza and what you absolutely won't eat. Beer or Cokes?

Everything, anything. Will not eat anchovies or sliced tomatoes. Beer.

I typed *OMY*, and the phone auto corrected to *on my way*, when I hit *Send*. I continued to stare at the conversation, waiting to see if she replied. After a few moments of nothing, I figured she'd turned her phone off like she had last time.

For some reason, I had been thinking about getting her a little something. Not as a Valentine's gift, but because if anyone deserved a little present in their life, it was Kenzie. It had to be something that would be useful to her or she wouldn't accept it. I couldn't show up with a new phone or announce that I would add her to my phone plan. That was too controlling, crossing boundaries she was struggling to keep in place. For someone with so little, she protected what was hers fiercely. She hadn't given up when it would be easier to do so.

I knew what I was going to get her.

I put my phone in my pocket and grabbed my coat.

My first stop was the drugstore. They had a kiosk of prepaid phone cards. I selected one, and then as I approached the checkout counter, I got a tickle on the back of my neck. The hairs there stood on end. I cast my gaze around the store as I rubbed the back of my neck.

I wouldn't call it premonition, but it was a feeling I had before that told me to pay attention. I needed to look around and see if I was missing something important.

A large Trojans poster hung in the back near the pharmacy. The nerves along my spine settled down as if to say, 'Here is your clue, dumbass.' I wasn't going over to Kenzie's for a date or a hookup. I was going to keep a sad friend company. Something I'd done plenty of times without needing condoms. But none of my soldiers I had sat up with on long, dark nights were Kenzie.

More importantly, Kenzie wasn't one of my soldiers. She was a beautiful woman, and my libido was screaming for me to pick up a box of condoms already.

Beer, condoms, a box of chocolates, and a phone card. It looked like I was preparing for a date. I slid my credit card into my wallet after paying for it all. "What's the best pizza place around here?" I asked the cashier. I really hoped she wasn't going to say the place out by the highway. I'd had their pizza before. I wasn't a fan.

"Tommy-Oh's, but they don't deliver," she said.

Tommy-Oh's sounded familiar. "That's the place downtown, by the hardware store, right?"

"That's the place. I don't think you'll be able to get a table there tonight. But they do take-out. I'd call ahead if I were you."

"Thanks, I will," I said as I grabbed the case of beer and my small paper bag.

Back in the truck, I pulled out my phone. I more than half hoped Kenzie had texted me again. I liked her texts. But I understood why she hadn't. Well, hopefully, my little gift would change that.

I looked up the number for Tommy-Oh's and called.

"We aren't taking reservations for tonight, the wait is already an hour, and if you want to order to-go, we're only doing larges. Your choices are cheese margherita, pepperoni with extra cheese, veggie lovers', and the kitchen sink. If you don't like it, don't order. What can I do for you?"

"Give me one pepperoni and one kitchen sink. Pay now or when I get there?"

"Nice and decisive. Pay when you pick up. Name?"

"Tate."

"See you in twenty, Tate."

That had probably been the easiest pizza ordering I had ever done. But what was I going to do for twenty minutes? It was only a ten-minute drive across town to pick up the pizza.

Thirty minutes later, I was taking the steps two at a time to get to Kenzie's apartment.

"You brought beer?" she asked as she opened the door.

"What, no 'hi'?"

"Hi, Tate. Did you bring beer?"

"I did," I said as I set everything down on her kitchen table.

She tore open the case and popped open a can without even noticing the brand. She tipped her head back and began pouring the beer down her throat.

"Whoa, whoa, whoa!" I reached out for her and snagged the can out of her hand before she completely drained it. "That's beer, not water. Have you even eaten anything today?"

She wiped her mouth with the back of her arm. "No, but that's what the pizza is for."

She opened the top box and inhaled appreciatively. "You got Tommy-Oh's." She slid a slice of the kitchen sink pizza, with everything on it, out of the box and folded it in half lengthwise. She put at least a third of the slice into her mouth before she bit down.

"You aren't drunk, are you?" I asked.

"No, but I want to be."

"You called me over here to get you drunk?" I was a touch annoyed because I thought she had wanted my company.

She turned and finally looked at me. Her eyes were red like she hadn't stopped crying all afternoon.

"Oh, Kenzie. Come here." I pulled her against my chest. She was hurting badly today.

"I want this pain to go away. I miss them so much. And this fucking day always comes back and reminds me of all of it. I can't get away from Valentine's Day. I hate it, Tate. I hate it."

"So you want to get drunk to forget?"

She nodded. "I don't know how else to make it go away. I can't sleep, and I know that a few beers and I'll get drunk enough to sleep and forget."

"Drinking is not your answer, Kenzie. That's a slippery slope it's best to just not approach. Alcoholics Anonymous is full of Army vets. You don't want to forget that way."

She felt good in my arms. I was a serious jerk for thinking the thoughts I was while she struggled with her emotions. But if it took my holding her all night to help her, I would be here.

"What am I supposed to do?" she asked.

"We could try a distraction," I suggested.

"Like what?"

"A movie? We could play poker," I suggested. I was going to need a distraction soon if she kept wiggling around against my chest the way she was. I could feel the warmth of her breasts pressed against me. And damn it, I was far too aware of her thigh brushing against mine.

"I tried a movie, but I can't focus."

I looked down at her. Her big eyes cast up to me. I took her sharp little chin in my fingers and tilted her face up to meet mine. Only her words could have stopped me, and I didn't want her to say anything.

I slid my lips across hers.

She hummed, or maybe it was me, and then she was wrapping her arms around my neck. I leaned into her, scooping my hands over and around, and then finally under that glorious ass of hers before lifting her up.

She squeaked into my mouth but kept kissing me. Her tongue was the sweetest ambrosia on the planet. I carried her to the couch and kept a grip on her and lowered until she was on top and I was sinking into the cushions.

"We could always give you new, better memories for today," I managed when she pulled back and stared down at me.

I struggled out of my coat and then tore my shirt off. If I was going to make any new memories with Kenzie tonight, I wanted to feel her against my skin.

She just kept looking at me.

"We don't have to do anything you don't want to do," I said.

"What if I want to do it all?"

"I'm willing to oblige. But you're in control here, Kenzie. If you say no at any point, I will stop. If you tell me to leave, I will leave."

"If I tell you to make love to me?" She looked so nervous, but she held steady, her eyes wide. And she kept licking her lips like she wanted to taste me again.

A wide grin crossed my face. "I brought condoms."

16

KENZIE

With Tate's lips on mine, I couldn't remember anything. His touch took away the pain. I didn't want memories anymore, and I wanted his hands on my body.

He tore his shirt off, and it was all I could do not to start rubbing my face all over him like a scent marking cat.

"Seriously?" I couldn't believe he was not only willing to have sex with me, but he was prepared.

"I mean, yeah. I didn't come over here expecting anything. It was an opportunistic purchase, that's all."

"That's all?" I started laughing. What were the odds that he just happened to get the best pizza in town and show up with condoms? I had been half-joking when I said those words, but now, it seemed destined to happen.

I started to fight my shirt off over my head. Tate helped, holding me in place so I maintained my balance and then pulling the shirt from my arms. He made a low, guttural sound as I sat there perched on his knees, looking down at him. I lowered back down, pressing my nearly naked breasts into his bare chest.

His skin was on fire, or maybe mine was. I never expected his skin to feel so smooth and soft against mine. He was all muscle, and I was the polar opposite. My squish and extra portion-sized bits didn't seem to bother him at all. After all, he had lifted me and carried me to the couch without a single complaint.

His hands were large. He grabbed and kneaded at my skin, grabbing my leg, then my butt. I sucked in a startled gasp when he palmed my breast and began to run this thumb in circles over my nipple. It felt right, his hands on me, his lips on mine. And that's what I focused on, how right everything felt, including the hard bulge that had developed between us.

Tate was getting a hard-on because of me. That was a powerful feeling.

He reached between us and cupped me through my jeans. I had never allowed anyone to get close enough to touch me the way he was. The way he made me feel, I was glad I had waited for him. I mimicked the gesture and ran my hand over the hard ridge at the front of his jeans. I could feel the shape of him through the fabric. His cock was hot, hotter than the rest of him.

"Condoms are in the bag," he groaned.

I looked over the back of the couch at the pizza boxes on the table. Bag? I saw it.

He unfastened his belt and opened his pants, putting his cock into my hand. I stopped moving with the shock of it. He had literally just handed me his cock. It was thick and heavy. I ran my thumb over the tip and wiped away a drip of his arousal. He felt like suede, or velvet wrapped over granite. Somehow, it was soft and lush but hard and dangerous all at once.

"You keep stroking me like that, and it will go off," he said. His voice was thick and gravelly.

"That's the goal, right?" I teased.

"Go get the condoms. I want to be inside you, woman," he ordered.

My toes curled, and my knees forgot how to work. I was stuck in place perched on his legs, looking between us, stroking his glorious manhood. This was all too fantastical to be real. He smacked my ass.

I looked up into his eyes in startled shock.

He laughed.

"Condoms," I eventually repeated. I scrambled off his lap, a little less gracefully than I would have liked at the moment. I returned with the bag and handed it to him.

He shoved his hand inside and pulled out a box of condoms. He tossed the bag and tore into the box. I stood there watching him as he ripped the foil pack with his teeth and rolled the condom down his length. Every movement he took caused something on my body to clench or tingle, wishing he were touching me instead of me watching him.

"Hey, are you going to help me out here?"

I shook my head and then started nodding. "You look like you've got it well in hand."

"I'd rather it be in your hands." He smoldered at me.

I must have blushed or looked shocked because he started laughing. "Kenzie, I can't do this with you if you're going to stand way over there with your clothes on."

He sat up and reached for me, grabbing my jeans by the waistband and pulling me a few steps closer. With dexterity, he opened the button and unzipped my jeans. I finally figured out what I was supposed to do. I helped him push my jeans off, and then I kicked them the rest of the way off.

I should have been cold or nervous. I was completely naked with a man. I was naked with Tate. Time to freak out was long past. He held his hand out to me and helped me back onto the couch, straddling his lap. His mighty cock sat between us, poking me in the belly.

I leaned into him, running my hands over his chest and finding his mouth with mine. His hands ran over my skin. I shuddered when he cupped me again, only this time, there were no clothes between his fingers and my pussy.

Electricity shot into me when he slid his fingers into my folds and hit that bundle of nerves. Oh, God, did that feel good. I moaned and wiggled my hips, wanting him to touch me like that again. I didn't look, I just wanted to feel and let him do what he was doing.

His finger was replaced with something wider, softer. I realized he was brushing his cock over my sensitive areas. That felt amazing. Tate knew exactly what he was doing, which was a good thing because I felt like I was making this up as I went along.

I whimpered when he pressed the tip against my opening. This was it. This was the moment where I went from virgin to not. Where I went from never knowing what a man felt like to having full carnal knowledge. It felt like a moment loaded with importance, yet somehow, not having any, all at once.

Why had I waited so long? I clearly didn't care whether Tate was in love with me or not, and yet I had never allowed myself to be in this position before.

"You still good?" Tate's voice was low and quiet.

"Yeah, just enjoying you," I said. It was true. There was more going on in my head, but at the moment, it was nothing more than noise getting in the way.

Tate's fingers bit into my hips, pulling me down as he thrust up. He filled me. I gasped at the suddenness of it. This was why. He was why I had waited. I needed someone as perfect as him to take me here for the first time. I may have been perched above him, but he had full control of me and the situation. He pulled back only to thrust into me again.

My ability to focus, to think left me stranded in a sea of nerves and feeling. My body was electricity, and Tate's drove shocks into me, set me ablaze, and sparked lightning. I couldn't see, I could barely breathe. I grasped his shoulders and rode him. I was useless as I held on. He had complete possession of me.

I screamed as my body wound up, and I felt my inner walls grab onto him, clutch at him. Something pulsed. I don't know if it was me or him, but it was amazing. And then it got better. Everything around me exploded. I crashed back against him, and he folded around me. I'm not sure how anything worked, but there were yells, and cheers, and more explosions, and then Tate was cradling me in his arms.

"Let's get you to bed." His voice was soothing and soft.

I was surrounded by his warmth, and then I must have fallen asleep.

Tate's thrashing woke me. I sat up. Whatever he was dreaming, it had a hold on him.

"Tate, wake up." I shook his shoulder.

He muttered something in his sleep and grabbed my arm. He tried to pull me. He wasn't very strong or effective in his sleep, but I ended up draped over his chest.

"Tate, stop, wake up!"

He sat bolt upright. I fell into his lap. He looked down at me, fear in his face. A second later, he relaxed as he recognized me and figured out where he was.

"I didn't hurt you, did I? I'm sorry. I should go." He swung his legs out of bed.

"Because you had a bad dream or because you slept with me?" I asked. A knot of fear formed in my gut. "You aren't leaving because you regret last night, do you?"

He stopped and turned to me. Damn, he was glorious, like a Greek statue come to life. He shook his head. A smile slowly formed on his lips.

"Why would I regret last night?"

"Because I'm a… was a virgin," I confessed.

His smile dropped away. He slid back onto the bed. "Kenzie, you should have said something."

"Why? I figured you could tell." I shrugged. I certainly had been able to tell.

He shook his head. "First times together can be awkward, and I wasn't paying attention because I wasn't expecting it. I would have taken extra care, made sure it was everything you wanted."

I reached out and put my hand on his chest. "It was. It was exactly what I needed."

He picked up my hand and kissed my fingers. "What does this change for you, other than the obvious? Do you expect us to start dating, or was that a one-time stress response?"

I blushed. I hadn't thought about what sleeping with Tate would mean in the greater scheme of things. "I'm not really sure what came over me. After all, I wasn't drunk. But I forgot the pain, and I have a much nicer memory for Valentine's Day now. Can we be friends while I figure out what's going on in my head? And whatever you do, do not let Ruby know you spent the night."

"Cross my heart." He made the X motion over his chest. "Kenzie, I have zero regrets. I'm honored you chose me."

He pulled me into his arms and stretched out, pulling the covers back over us. "I was leaving because I didn't want you upset because of my bad dream."

"I know a thing or two about bad dreams," I confessed. "I'm glad you're staying."

17

TATE

"Are you stalking me? You know Kenzie doesn't like it when I accept rides home from strange men," Ruby quipped as she climbed into the truck. She was nothing if not consistent. Sarcasm was her natural language.

"And yet, here you are, voluntarily getting in for a ride home," I joked right back.

"It's hardly voluntary. Kenzie left a message at the office telling me you were gonna pick me up today. Do I have a doctor's appointment or something?"

I shook my head and let the truck inch forward in the after school pick-up traffic. "She said I had to ask you directly. Are you interested in a job?"

I must have stunned Ruby into silence. She said nothing but stared at me. "I'm not old enough for a job. Have to be at least fourteen, and I'm only thirteen."

"I'm not talking about a regular job with timecards. I'm talking about helping me out around my house. I have a barn that needs cleaning out."

"And you're going to pay me? Actually pay me cash?" she said as if she had worked jobs before where she had been paid in ways that hadn't involved money.

"If cash is what you want. Or we can deposit money straight into your savings account. If you want me to pay you in certificates of deposit and savings bonds, we'll have to make a spreadsheet to track your hours. But my intention is cash, and shopping."

"When you say shopping, what do you mean?" She clearly didn't trust me.

I shrugged. "Uh, say you want a PlayStation. We figure out how many hours of work that is. You do the work, we go shopping and buy a PlayStation."

"Really?" That had gotten her attention.

"So, am I taking you to my place to show you around, or am I taking you to the library to do homework?"

"Your place!"

I drove to the Burger Jeff first.

"This isn't your place," Ruby complained as I put the truck in park.

"Observant. I keep telling Kenzie you're smart. I want your sister to know where you are. Do you want some fries? I'm buying."

Kenzie smiled as she saw us approach the counter.

"You're not cleaning," I pointed out.

"Not until after breaks. Do you two have a deal?" Kenzie asked as she punched an order into the computer system.

"We do." I held out my credit card to pay, but she placed her hand over mine and pushed it away with a shake of her head. I'd let her comp us some fries and drinks as long as it wasn't coming out of her pay.

"Do you have your phone with you?"

"Kenzie never carries that thing," Ruby interjected.

"I do, but it's not on," Kenzie admitted.

"I want to be able to text you. I'm paying for it. We talked about this," I started.

"Since when are you paying for our phone?" Ruby asked indignantly.

"Since I realized how tightly budgeted your sister is. I want to text her, so I'm willing to cover that cost. I gave her a phone card the other day."

"Why didn't you tell me?" Ruby pleaded.

"Because it's between me and Tate. I have the phone, and it's off while I'm at work. I'll turn it on when I take my next break."

I nodded. That was acceptable. "I'm going to text you my address and instructions for getting to the house. Come over after work. I'm making dinner."

"You're almost as bossy as Ruby," Kenzie teased as she handed me the bag with fries. Ruby took the cups and filled them at the self-service machine.

"It's called commanding. Hazard of the old job. Please, let me make dinner for you tonight. Besides, I want you to see where Ruby will be most days after school."

"She has homework," Kenzie started.

"I will make sure she does it. I understand priorities. School first."

"Ugh, you sound like Kenzie. *School is important.*" Ruby mocked us.

My chest tightened when Kenzie smiled and waved as we left. I wanted her to come with us and never have to be stuck in that place again. I hated the idea that Mac could walk in and start talking to her at any moment.

"If you're paying for phone minutes, does that make you and Kenzie—"

"Friends," I cut her off before she could say anything else. It didn't matter what I wanted. Until Kenzie felt comfortable with what was happening between us, we were friends.

Hopefully, friends with extended benefits. I could not stop thinking about the other night. It had not been a date because Kenzie didn't date. But whatever she wanted to call it, I called it fucking amazing, and I wanted to revisit the feeling of her skin against me again.

I took a long drink, needing the cold soda to wash away the hot thoughts that were demanding attention.

"Can I get a phone?"

"What?"

"If you're willing to pay for minutes for Kenzie, do you think I could get a phone with the money you're going to pay me?"

"I can't see why not. Kenzie will have to decide whether you're old enough and all that kind of shit—sorry, stuff."

Ruby laughed. "Just don't let Kenzie hear you drop the F-bomb, or she'll make you clean the kitchen."

"Noted."

Ruby munched on her fries as I finished the short drive to the house.

"Holy moly, you live here?" She climbed out of the truck after I put it in park and shut off the engine. Her big eyes were glued to the front of the house.

I guess it was impressive. I probably looked at it with some form of awe the first time I pulled up. It was a multi-storied Victorian style with a wrap-around front porch, a tower, and lots of crenelation and decorative moulding. But it was weather worn, and the front stairs were noticeably off plumb. One of the dormers also listed to the side.

Ruby looked like she saw magic and potential. All I saw was a growing to-do list, and that was just the outside.

"What do you want me to do? Clean this?"

I gestured toward the back. "I really need help out back, in the barn. It's full of junk. And tools, but it's all so piled in, it might as well be junk."

"Good, I hate cleaning bathrooms," she said as she returned to the truck and dragged her backpack and skateboard out.

"Come on, I'll show you where you can put your stuff." I jogged up the stairs and opened the door.

Once inside, her expression of awe quickly vanished. Inside, the glamor of potential was replaced with the reality of old furniture and layers of dust. "It's not as bad as it was. I'm making progress. It's slow going but it's going. This way."

I led her through the kitchen, where I told her to put her things, and then out the back door. We crossed the yard, and I hauled open the sliding barn door.

"Whoa, you weren't kidding. I'm so getting a phone. Not to be rude, but this is a lot of work. Are you sure you can pay me?"

"Don't worry about that. I can afford to pay you. The real question is, do you think you can handle this?"

"As long as you don't expect me to get it all done today."

I laughed. Her sarcasm was on point.

"There is a lot of wood in here. Just boards and planks and blocks of it. And it's all over the place. I think" —I pointed toward the ceiling where an old-fashioned line shaft pole was installed— "this was some kind of workshop. All of that is how they used to power tools before electricity. There's probably a steam generator or something to drive it, but it's buried in all of this. I want to spend a couple of hours today piling up wood."

"Do you want it sorted or anything?" Ruby asked.

I shook my head. "We can sort it later. I wouldn't even know how to sort what's here."

Ruby got right to work. I cleared an area next to the door, and she began piling up all the pieces she could get to and drag over without help. When she found a piece too big, she called me over. Some of the wood was definitely high-quality and would be valuable to the right person.

"These are skis." Ruby held up matching planks.

"Looks like wood to me."

"Seriously? These are vintage skis. Look how long they are."

She held up the long, slender skis that I had mistaken for more random planks of wood.

"Those are skis?" I crossed to where she stood and took them from her. "They're good quality, but long."

"These are for soft snow."

"You ski?" I asked.

"Ski-board. You can't live around here and not ski. I mean, we have ski days at school, where the whole school goes. Do you ski?"

I nodded. "Absolutely. How about Kenzie?"

"Yeah, she used to ski. She hasn't in a long time. I haven't been since last year."

"How long before you're allowed to go skiing again?" I pointed at her wrist.

She lifted her arm. "This has no impact on whether I go skiing or not. I don't use my wrist to ski. We're broke, and lift passes are not cheap."

"Do you think you and Kenzie would want to go skiing with me sometime?"

"Seriously? You'd take us skiing? Wait, that's not going to come out of my pay? Because I'd rather have a phone."

"Hey, Bowers, you here? Major?"

I looked at Ruby as someone called my name.

"In here!" I yelled, turning toward the door.

I watched the silhouette of a man drop a duffel bag and step into the darker confines of the barn before I recognized him.

"Major Bowers, it's Allan Calder, Sir. You said I should come find you if I—" He stopped when he saw Ruby.

"Calder, welcome. Come on in. This is my friend, Ruby. Ruby, this is Allan. He was one of my soldiers in the Army."

18

KENZIE

I wiggled my toes around in the rented ski boots. They were a little squished, but I could still feel them. That was good. My skis swayed back and forth. I practiced getting them into position before the lift reached back to the top of the mountain.

I turned around and waved at Tate behind us.

"I can't believe Tate brought us on a surprise ski day. Did you know about this?" I asked Ruby.

I could barely see my sister bundled up under all of her gear.

She shook her head. "I told you. I found some ancient skis in that shack behind the house, and then Tate asked me when your next day off was. That's it. I had no idea."

"Uh-huh, you didn't convince him that he needed to take us skiing? What did you say to him, exactly?"

"Kenzie, chill out. I did not pester Tate to take us skiing. He asked if I skied. So, duh, I told him I ski-boarded and that you skied. I may have mentioned that I hadn't been skiing since last year's school ski day, but I didn't do anything."

I didn't know if I believed her. I knew how persistent Ruby could be. I wasn't mad about it. I liked skiing too. The biggest part of my concern was that I let Tate convince me that skipping a day of school wouldn't hurt Ruby's grades. It was just one day. There was no way I was going to go skiing without her, so I gave in.

The lift got close to the top. I focused on getting my skis facing forward. I didn't want to be that person again. I had already fallen flat on my ass the first time I tried to get off the lift today.

I had successfully entertained Tate and the guys running the lift when I slid from the chair to my feet to my butt and couldn't stop laughing. I didn't want to fall again. My ability to be the cool ski bunny was shot. Falling negated the image. I was far from cool and graceful.

I was the fat, clumsy chick. I had to own it. It was so embarrassing. I used to dominate on this mountain. I was on it every week my junior and senior years of high school. I was that jerk child who labeled other skiers as slope bunnies and clumsy chicks.

My fat butt… well, I always had extra padding for falling. That wasn't my issue. It was the falling. I didn't want Tate to see me as some pitiful, untalented idiot on skis. And I hated that I was basically handing Ruby all the fodder she would need to harass me for the next ten years.

She was graceful and smooth. She boarded, on snow and on wheels, better than she walked.

My first run down the mountain had been slow. There was muscle memory buried in the depths of my thighs that needed reawakening. Ruby literally lapped me, sliding past me a second time while I was still winding my way down.

Tate went even slower than I had. At first, I thought he was new on the slopes. No, he was trying to be nice.

Jerk.

"Second time's a charm," I said as I watched the approaching dismount. I pulled my goggles over my eyes. With a little hop, I was out of the seat and on my feet.

The guys running the lift had their hands out to help. I grabbed onto the guy's offered hand. "You got it," he said.

I slid out of the way and waited for Tate.

"See you later!" Ruby called out as she landed on her board and leaned into the slope. She was off like a shot, zigzagging around other slow-pokes like me.

Tate dismounted like some kind of Olympic athlete.

"Are you ready?" he asked.

"Are you going to mock me all the way down again?" I lifted my goggles and glared at him.

"I wasn't mocking you, Kenzie."

"You totally were. You kept going super slow and just stayed behind me."

He laughed. "I was enjoying the view."

I looked around at the trees and the snow and the side of the mountain. The sky was a beautiful clear blue color. He was right, it was a really pretty day.

"It is beautiful out here," I agreed.

"I wasn't talking about the scenery, Kenzie. Your ass in those snow pants is a sight to behold." He leaned over, smacked me in the butt, and then went swish-swish-swish down the slope like he was born on skis.

Mocking me.

I no longer went swish-swish. My thighs couldn't remember. My knees didn't want to stay bent. I went groaning and complaining. This was harder than it should have been. Especially when I used to be really good at skiing.

I was the slowest person on the slope, being passed by kids barely big enough to walk zipping past me on their triangle-shaped trainer skis. I didn't want to even think about the kids on the snowboards. They all looked like munchkins from the 'merry old land of Oz'. It wasn't fair.

I pouted my way down the slope, wiping my cold nose on the back of my sleeve.

Tate in his mountainous glory of height was easy to spot at the bottom of the slope. I eased up close to him, too aware of how awkward I was when he grabbed my arm. Five years earlier, I would have snow plowed right up to him and sprayed him with powder.

"Where's Ruby?"

"She's on her way back up. You doing okay?" he asked.

"It was easier the last time I did this. How come you're so good?"

"I grew up skiing."

"I did too, but I'm out here like somebody's grandma, afraid to fall and break a hip. You took off like some downhill speed demon." I might have whined a little too much. I was trying to joke, but it came out all wrong.

Tate didn't exactly stick out his tongue, but he placed the tip of his tongue against his upper lip as he leaned in close. He let out a heavy breath. "Kenzie, sweetheart. You aren't exactly all that active."

I rolled my eyes. I put my hand on his chest and pushed him away. "I walk. Are you saying I'm fat?" I mastered the teasing tone I had been trying for.

Tate looked me up and down, and I swear he swiped drool out of the corner of his mouth with his thumb. I felt that look in my core as if he had scanned me with his hands and not his eyes.

"You say fat, I say delicious. I meant no insult to your shape, which I find extremely beguiling, but rather to the strength of your muscles. We can go slow, and hopefully, you'll want to come skiing again with me. Build up that strength."

"Are you flirting with me?" I asked.

"Hell yes, I am. I didn't bring you out here to cause you any kind of physical or mental distress," he said.

"No? Then why did you bring us skiing?"

"To show off. You grew up on and off these slopes. I can't imagine that you would want a man who didn't know how to ski."

He had a point. But skiing had fallen off my list of what was important five years ago. I never thought I'd have an opportunity for it to become important to me again.

"I think I can take it one more time," I admitted, looking up at all the skiers making their way down to the rest area where we stood.

"Shall we?" Tate escorted me to the lift.

The ride up was easy, fun. Tate made me laugh.

"So, you brought me out here to show off. But did I pass your test? You can ski, yay. But apparently, I can't anymore. Does that score me lower on your tally sheet?"

"Kenzie, you are already perfect on my tally sheet."

I laughed. "This mountain air is making you delusional."

"Not delusional, but I am looking forward to snuggling under blankets with hot chocolate after we get home."

"Are you forgetting there's a thirteen-year-old who will be in between us?" I pointed out that Ruby would be there.

"Is she clueless, or purposefully acting like a chaperone?" Tate asked.

"A little of both."

About halfway down, Ruby passed us again.

"Wait up!" Tate called before jumping and gaining speed.

He waited for me a few hundred yards down hill. "I told her this was your last run and to go ahead and do another run if she wanted, but to meet us in the lodge when she was done."

"Don't you want to do another run with her?" I asked.

"I'm showing off for you, Kenzie. That means after displaying my skills on the slopes, I have to get you hot chocolate by a fire. That way, you know I'm a package deal."

"You're crazy, Tate. You know that, right?"

He guided me down to the lodge, staying with me the whole way when I knew he wanted to go faster downhill. I knew I would have wanted to go faster.

"You losers ready to go already?" Ruby found us about an hour later in the lounge area of the lodge. I had my stockinged feet propped on a footrest and my hands wrapped around an almost empty mocha.

"That was not one more run," I pointed out.

"So I went twice." Ruby shrugged. "Sue me."

"I'll make you clean the kitchen after dinner," I said.

"You can clean my kitchen. Dinner at my place," Tate said. "Let's go turn your gear in."

I watched as they walked back to the rental office. Even though I felt physically unable to keep up, I really enjoyed today. It felt like what life used to be like and not what my life had become, all work and worry.

19

TATE

There was something very special about arriving back at the house and having it all lit up while having Ruby and Kenzie's laughter accompany me through the cold air from the truck and into the warmth of the kitchen.

"Damn, that smells good! Calder, what are you making?" I called out as I stepped inside.

Ruby charged through the kitchen and into the front of the house. She had only been working for me for a few days, but she was already comfortable being in the house. Kenzie hung back by the door. She wasn't comfortable in my space yet.

I wanted her to be as comfortable as possible. I wanted her here. My plans of treating her to a homemade meal earlier in the week were foiled by Allan's arrival. Fortunately, she understood. Unfortunately, that meant this was her first time inside.

"You have a good day on the slopes?" Allan asked. He looked at Kenzie directly.

I felt a growl form in my chest. He needed to not be looking at her.

"I don't know if a good day is the right way to describe it." Kenzie chuckled.

"We had a fun day," I said a little more aggressively than necessary.

"Uh-oh, did I step on another land mine?" Allan said.

I gave him a very pointed look. He laughed and waggled his eyebrows.

"Nothing so drastic," Kenzie said, oblivious of his double meaning. She stepped into the kitchen properly and finally took her coat off. "Apparently, I have completely forgotten how to ski. I'm going to be so sore in the morning," Kenzie said.

"Then you"—Allan pointed at me with finger guns— "should take her into the other room and rub her feet or something while I finish dinner. It should be ready in about twenty minutes."

The growl in my chest relaxed. He knew who Kenzie was to me, and this was his way of letting me know.

"Don't you need any help getting everything ready?" Kenzie asked.

"Not from you. Send Ruby back if she's willing to help out," he said.

I tilted my head to Kenzie, indicating we should leave. She followed me out to the living room. There were other downstairs rooms, but I hadn't finished cleaning everything out. But the living room was clean, and I had replaced the furniture with comfortable modern styles.

"Did I say something to get banished?" Kenzie asked.

I sat on the corner of the couch, expecting her to sit next to me. She flopped down in the side chair.

"I can't rub your feet from there." I patted the couch next to me.

"He was just saying that—"

"He was just saying that to let me know he was simply talking to you, and not flirting. Get over here and let me flirt with you."

"You're incorrigible," she said. But she came and sat next to me. She kicked off her shoes and curled up with her head on my shoulder. "You don't have to rub my feet, at least not right now."

Ruby stepped into the living room, looked at us, then looked at the TV. "You know, the TV has to be on to watch a movie."

I laughed. "We're getting warm before dinner. Allan said he could use your help." I hitched my thumb over my shoulder, kicking her out of the living room.

Allan's announcing dinner came far too soon. Kenzie slipped off the couch and shoved her feet back into her shoes. The table was set, and Ruby carried in the salad as Allan carried in the roast.

"Oh, everything smells so good," Kenzie purred.

It did smell good. It tasted even better.

"When did you learn how to cook?" I asked before shoving more of the garlic roasted potatoes into my mouth.

"Part of my recuperation. I was encouraged to take up a hobby, and I like to eat. Seemed like a win-win."

"Were you injured?" Kenzie asked.

Allan paused. We made eye contact. I waited for his signal. I could deflect, or he could continue. This was his call.

"Yeah, I got hurt in the Army."

"Is that why you didn't come skiing with us?" Ruby asked.

"No, I can't ski. I couldn't ski before the accident, but I really can't ski now." He reached down and knocked on his left calf. It made a hollow thunking sound.

"You have a fake leg?" Ruby asked enthusiastically.

"Ruby!" Kenzie said through clenched teeth.

"It's okay. Yeah, I have a prosthetic lower leg."

"Can I see it?"

"Ruby!"

Allan waved Kenzie's concern away. "Not at dinner. But sure, I'll show you sometime."

"Did you know each other in the Army?" Kenzie asked.

"I served under the major in the Middle East. At least until this happened, and then he retired."

Kenzie got quiet. She looked down at her food and nodded.

I put my hand on hers. "You okay?"

Her eyes met mine. "Scary, that's all. I didn't mean to bring up bad memories."

"Oh, no, not bad memories at all. Sure, the active-duty part wasn't ideal, but I loved my time in the service. I had brothers by my side all the time. It was great, like living with your best friends. It was great, and the hard parts, well, you didn't go through them alone."

"But you got hurt, like seriously hurt," Ruby pointed out.

"Yeah, I went and stepped on an incendiary. I loved being there with my guys, but it was dangerous."

"Allan thought he was at some kind of party camp on his last tour. Always arranging cookouts and ballgames," I remembered.

"Well, the food sucked, I had to do something." He laughed.

Those were the good memories. Those were the ones to hold on to. And not the ones that visited me in my nightmares.

After dinner, Ruby stepped in and offered to clean up. Maybe she had accepted this as her punishment for taking an extra run on the slope and wasn't going to argue, or maybe she was just being helpful. She had a smart mouth on her, but underneath that attempt at a tough exterior, she was a good kid.

We waited until she and Allan were finished before starting a movie. I wanted to keep Kenzie by my side longer, and a movie to wrap up our day seemed like a good idea.

"I'm turning in. Night. Nice to finally meet you, Kenzie. 'Night, Major."

"Good night, Allan." Turning to Ruby, I asked, "Do we need popcorn?"

"How can you still be hungry? I'm stuffed. We do not need popcorn, but I wouldn't say no to ice cream."

I shook my head. "I'll be right back."

I had enough ice cream for one bowl. Lucky kid, it was hers. I tossed a bag of popcorn into the microwave and made a mug of hot chocolate for Kenzie and grabbed a beer for myself.

Ruby still stole a handful of my popcorn as I handed her the bowl of ice cream.

"Thank you," Kenzie said, looking up at me with eyes that seemed to be bigger and more luminous in the low light of the living room.

At some point during the movie, Ruby passed out.

"Leave her," Kenzie said. She sounded sleepy. "I'll wake her up when the movie is over. We can go home then."

"You could stay," I suggested.

Kenzie didn't say anything as she looked at me. She snuggled against my chest a little closer as we watched the rest of the movie. I couldn't pay attention and eagerly waited for the end credits to roll.

"Come on." I grabbed Kenzie's hand and pulled her from the couch.

I scooped Ruby up. She snorted. "Still asleep?" I asked. I couldn't see her face once I had a grip on her.

"She's still out cold."

Kenzie followed me up the stairs and into the second guest room. I put Ruby on the bed and stepped away. Kenzie pulled off her sister's shoes.

"So, this is a twin bed. There really isn't room for me to sleep in here," she pointed out.

I nodded.

"I can't sleep with you. Allan and Ruby would know."

"Allan already knows there is something between us. And Ruby doesn't need to know the details. My bedroom is on the far end of the hall." I held my hand out to her.

She looked down at her sleeping sister and chewed on her lower lip. With a nod, she put her hand in mine.

"I don't have any pajamas with me."

"You aren't going to need pajamas tonight," I replied as I led her into my room.

"Tate." My name was an admonition. I was in trouble.

"You can sleep in one of my shirts. You'll look adorable. I promise I won't do anything you don't approve of." I wanted to do quite a lot to her, and I was certain, once I was able to get my hands and mouth on her body, she would approve of it all.

I pulled a shirt out of my dresser and handed it to Kenzie and showed her the bathroom. While she got ready, I stripped down and put on a pair of long flannel sleep pants. I was in bed when she came back into the room. She was adorable. My shirt strained at her breasts and fell to her bare thighs. She still had socks on her feet.

She hovered on the far side of the bed. I reached out to her and pulled her against my chest.

"Tate." Her voice was soft.

"Touch me, Kenzie. I want to feel your hands on me."

"I don't know what you want, where to start," she admitted.

I took her hand and placed it on my chest. "Just touch me, any way you want."

Her fingers were ticklish and curious. The night wasn't long enough to get my fill of her hands on me.

20

KENZIE

I hated my job. There was no way to convince myself otherwise. And I hated that after having a taste of what life was like through Tate's generosity that I was back dumping frozen fries into the deep fryer and wiping down plastic booth tables.

Without realizing it, he reminded me that there was more to being alive than the struggle of bills and surviving. And I wanted out of this bottomless well of despair that I had been living in.

I set the timer on the fries. Every time I tried to find a different job, I failed so epically, I stayed put. No matter how often I spoke to the owner, and applied, and hemmed dress after dress, I still couldn't get a job at the dress shop. And frankly, no one else wanted to hire full-time work and provide benefits. And we needed insurance. Ruby's broken wrist was proof of that.

My head started to throb. Maybe that's why I was feeling down. I had a headache. I went into the back and looked for some ibuprofen in my bag.

"Why aren't you out front?" Will asked.

I held up the bottle of pills as I fished it out of my bag and rattled it at him. "I have a headache."

"Oh, I thought you were hiding again," he said.

My spine lost any strength I had left, and I slumped forward. "Is Mac here? Can't you just take care of him and send him away?"

"Do your job, Kenzie. Or do we need to have a chat about your hours?"

I shut my mouth and pursed my lips. I tipped out an extra pill into my hand. I needed a couple for my head, and one just to deal with the pain that Will was being. Keeping the pills in my hand until I could grab a drink, I made my way back to the front of the restaurant. I filled a small cup with Coke at the drive-thru dispenser before finally being able to toss back the meds. I gave myself a moment to pray the pills would take effect immediately before heading back to my station.

I was doing the break rotation before I cleaned everything. "Are you ready for a break?" I asked Latisha.

"Will just gave me my break, sorry. Are you trying to avoid that old guy again?"

I nodded. I couldn't think of anything I could do. It was time to face my reality.

I opened a third register and told Jess to finish the order she was on and take a break.

"I can help you over here." I waved over the family that was next in Jess's line.

Mac stepped up to the counter. "I'll have my regular, Kenzie. You know what I like."

I looked at him with zero emotion. Partly because my head was starting to really hurt and partly because if I gave way to what I was thinking, I would start cussing him out. "Mac, you're not next in line. These people are. I will take your order when it's your turn."

"Kenzie," he started to complain.

"No." I said it with all the anger I felt toward him. I then turned a fake smile to the family waiting. They looked a little concerned. "Sorry about that, can I take your order?"

I took orders, processed payments, loaded up trays and paper bags, and generally was busy. It was good. I didn't have time to think about my headache. I was better because there wasn't time for Mac to do anything more than place an order and take his food.

Jess came back and it was Dougie's turn to take a break. The lines were getting smaller. Unfortunately, the rush would be over soon, and I would be finished cycling through breaks as soon as Dougie came back, and I would be out on the floor, cleaning up, sooner than I wanted.

I saw Allan come in before he saw me. He waited in line like everyone else and then smiled when he realized it was me behind the counter.

"Hi, Kenzie. Sorry I couldn't stay up and watch the movie with everyone. I'm learning to listen to my body and go to bed when I'm tired. You know, not push my limits. I don't have the same stamina I used to."

"Allan, hi. Is this for here or to go? Do you know what you want to order?" I asked first so that no one could accuse me of chatting when there was work to do.

If Will didn't see me and take issue, then a customer would complain, or Mac would. Because Mac made everything about him. If I was talking to anyone, it had better be about work or he would pester me. In the past, Mac had gone so far as to interrupt the conversation I was having to ask why I was talking to that person and not him.

"Yeah, here, double-bacon burger, no tomato."

"Do you want that as a meal deal or just the burger? Ruby fell asleep in the middle of the movie, so no worries. That dinner you made was delicious. Thank you."

Allan smiled and nodded. I think he understood what I was doing because he didn't skip a beat.

"Meal deal, large, please. You're welcome. If I had known I liked to cook and was good at it, I probably never would have joined up. Didn't think I had any skills or choices."

I let out a heavy sign before telling him his total. "I hear you on that. That's why I'm stuck here."

He handed me cash. I made change and handed it back. I filled his order and slid his tray across to him.

"Do you have a break coming up?" he asked.

I shook my head. "No break, but I'll be out on the floor cleaning in a few minutes. I can chat while I work."

I couldn't help but watch him walk. Now that I knew he had a prosthetic, I was curious whether it had been obvious and I was just blind, or... He had to have gone through hundreds of hours of physical therapy. The man walked with a pretty even gait.

Mac was back in my line before Dougie returned.

"What was that all about? Do you have a new boyfriend already?" Mac grumbled.

I closed my eyes and wished Mac would go away. He was still there when I opened my eyes again. "What can I get for you?"

"You know what I want, Kenzie. But you aren't on the menu."

Was he trying to be clever?

"You've already ordered lunch. Do you want a second order of fries, or do you want a sundae?"

"I want to know what you are smiling at that guy for. How do you think the big guy would react if he knew you were talking to another man?"

"There's a line behind you. You have to order or leave."

"Fries, give me fries. I don't eat ice cream."

I held out my hand for his payment. As long as he was a paying customer, Will let him harass me. As long as he was a paying customer, I couldn't tell him to fuck off like I really wanted to.

He paid and took his fries.

Dougie came back, and my stomach sank. Begrudgingly, I signed out of my register and went into the back for the cleaning supplies. I thought about hiding in the bathrooms, but Allan was still around, and I did want to talk to him. Maybe I could find out more about Tate and how he was like in the Army.

"Is everything okay?" I asked as I started to work on the booth behind Allan.

"It's a hamburger," he said. "But yeah, everything is fine. Hey. I hate to ask this. My leg is aching a lot today."

"Really? You don't even limp," I said.

"It takes a lot of effort to walk normally." He handed me a few dollars. "Could you get me a sundae?"

"Of course I can." I took the offered money and headed to the counter. I was covered in cleaning chemicals, so it was faster to have Dougie ring it up and put the sundae together.

Mac stepped in front of me as I carried a tray with a single sundae on it back to Allan. "This isn't that kind of restaurant."

He took the sundae and tossed it in the garbage.

"Mac, that wasn't yours." I turned to go back to get a second sundae made up.

"It was for your new boyfriend. How come you won't bring orders to me, Kenzie?"

I clenched my teeth. It wasn't my place to tell people Allan had a prosthetic leg. He clearly worked hard to appear like he didn't.

"Dougie, I need a second sundae. Mac, you need to leave." I finally said it, I finally told him to go. It was a relief, for a second, at least.

"Where's your manager?" Mac said in the loudest voice he had.

"You don't need to talk to Will. Mac, you're interfering with other people's orders."

Will showed up behind the counter. "What seems to be the problem here?"

"She can't tell me to leave. I'm a paying customer," Mac tattled on me like he was a toddler.

"Kenzie, we've talked about this. I'm sorry about her attitude. Kenzie, my office."

I slumped. I was defeated. Dougie slid a tray with the replacement sundae on it.

"Let me deliver this to an injured Army veteran." I emphasized each and every word so that Mac could understand. I delivered food when a customer needed assistance.

Mac's eyes went wide. I hoped he felt guilty. I grabbed the tray and brushed past him.

"Here you go." I slid the tray in front of Allan.

"You okay? Do I need to tell Tate about that guy? Or do you want me to handle him?"

I looked at Allan. His eyes looked glossy and a little wild. Not unlike Mac when he thought he was being treated unfairly.

"Tate knows about Mac. You only need to enjoy your ice cream," I said with a sigh.

21

TATE

"How did you figure this was a workshop?" Allan asked as he helped me to carry a thick plank of wood. "I think this might be teak."

"How would you know that?" I asked. To me, wood was wood.

"It looks like it. The color reminds me of furniture my mom has. She has a lot of Mid-Century teak stuff."

The color was a warm, orangey hue. We could see the color because at Ruby's snarky request, I put in a few LED work lights so we could see what we were actually doing.

"I vaguely remember being told that some of the pieces of old furniture I had grown up with were made by a great-grandfather, or something like that. Like I said, it's a vague memory. But what clinched it for me" —we dropped the plank onto a growing pile of larger rough, unrefined pieces— "is that system up there."

I pointed up. There were several flywheels and ratty looking scraps that I assumed were rotted out belts from a line shaft system.

"Fuck me, that's old shit. Like old, old. You think that still works?" Allan stared up with a squint.

I shrugged. "Basic machines can keep working as long as all the parts are there and not busted up. It would be interesting to restore the mechanics. I could probably sell the whole workshop to some collector at that point. I looked it up. The system is very simple. The shaft rotates and drives the flywheels of different machines. There could be all kinds of table saws, bench grinders, drills, who knows? Maybe even a lathe or other specialty tools."

"Would you even know what a lathe is if you saw one?" Allan chuckled.

"Probably not. But until we can get this cleared out, I wouldn't have any idea what's really in here." I continued to look up at the system. Based on the flywheels, I guessed there were at least four big pieces of equipment.

"Yeah, I hear you. Did they just shove everything from the house in here when they left?"

"It certainly seems like it. I don't know, there is still an awful lot of old furniture in the house. I haven't even started with the attic."

Allan looked out the open barn doors at the house. "Is there a cellar?"

"At least one. I found it when I went searching for the furnace."

"You have radiators. It's a boiler system, right?" he asked.

"Exactly. It fired up good to go, right away."

"It doesn't do a very good job. Your house is cold as fuck. At least my room is."

"That house is old as fuck. Remind me to take a look at your radiator later. My room and the downstairs get decently warm."

"That house is going to be really something when you're done with it," he said.

I nodded. It was. The question that had been lingering in the back of my mind whether I was going to keep it or not was settled now. At least as far as I was concerned. Maybe I should focus on the house and not the barn.

If I wanted someone else to move into the house with me—Allan didn't count—it needed to be in better condition. For starters, I should make sure all the radiators were functioning, and then get the furniture that is held together by dust and spiders out of the house.

"I'm wasting my time out here, aren't I?" I asked. I was mostly thinking out loud.

"Is that an existential question, or something more specific?" Allan asked for clarification.

"Maybe a little of both." I chuckled. "I was just wondering if maybe I should be focusing on working on the house."

"So, why are we out here?" Allan asked.

"Because every time I turn around, I need a tool. Like a crowbar, or a screwdriver. I'm at the hardware store every other day. You know, that's how I met Ruby, and then Kenzie."

"You met Ruby at the hardware store? What was a thirteen-year-old doing at the hardware store? And she introduced you to her sister? That kid is the best wingman you could ask for. They don't have another sister they're hiding, do they?"

I laughed. I really hadn't thought of Ruby as my wingman, but if she hadn't fallen… it's not like I would have walked in the Burger Jeff on my own.

"I never made it to the hardware store that day. Ruby wiped out in front of the truck. I scraped her off the pavement and took her to the ER. That's when she broke her wrist. I had no idea her older sister was as beautiful as she is." Kenzie was more than beautiful. She was fierce and determined. She struggled but tried really hard to not let Ruby see how unhappy it made her. And yet, she never hid the reality of their situation from Ruby, turning every misunderstanding into a learning opportunity. Kenzie was amazing in every way.

"What?" I turned back to Allan. "You say something?"

"I said you really like her."

"Yeah, I think I do," I admitted.

"You should know about the old guy bothering her at work, if you don't know about him already."

I groaned. I brushed my hand through my hair. "Yeah, I know about him."

"You want me to arrange an accident for him?"

I started to laugh but stopped and stared at Allan. Allan had been a party boy out on deployment. He played hard and he fought hard. Maybe too hard. He enjoyed all of it. I thought a lot of that would have changed after the incident.

Maybe it had, maybe it hadn't. I wouldn't have let him stay if I didn't trust him. After all, my previous self was capable of dangerous actions. I'm sure I could easily tap into that part of me again if needed.

"I'll take care of things with Mac. He's more of a pest than a threat. Thanks for the heads up."

"Kenzie really seemed bothered by him."

Something clenched in my chest. Allan had gotten to see her today and I hadn't. She may have been in my bed last night, but she and Ruby were up and out before I woke up.

"Hey, give me a hand with this shelf," Allan said. The topic of Mac was already gone and forgotten.

"Don't pull, it looks like it's stuck under—"

There was a crack, and then a rumble.

"Fuck!"

A cloud of dust swirled up into the air, and then the rumble got louder.

"Oh, shit!" Allan jumped back out of the way and the shelving unit collapsed.

He was on his ass and scrambling back as things continued to topple down. I got him under his armpits and dragged him out of the way.

"You good?" I asked.

He sat there nodding.

I panted from the adrenaline spike. "That was close."

I peered past the pile of rubble. "Check this out. There is a whole room back here."

I moved stuff around so I could climb past it into the room the collapse exposed. No wonder the barn felt jam-packed. A row of shelves, or maybe it had been a wall, created the smaller front space that someone had filled with everything Allan, Ruby, and I had already spent hours clearing away.

"What the hell?" Allan asked.

I turned back. He was back on his feet and watching me as I wandered around in the large, open space. Tarps covered several objects. I peeled one back. Dust launched into the air. I coughed and covered my mouth before pulling it back further. It was a piece of furniture. I removed another tarp from a second piece of furniture. "This must be stuff my grandfather never finished. This is really nice work."

Allan managed to climb over into the room. He ran his hand over the top of the first piece. "Did you see the inlay work done on this? Your grandfather did some amazing work. How come none of the furniture in the house is this nice?"

"That's a good question. The house had been sitting empty for quite a while when I got here. I think it's been at least twenty years since it had tenants. Maybe there were more pieces. Maybe that's what got moved to the East Coast all those years ago."

I continued to run my hands over the dresser I had uncovered. It wasn't a heavy, chunky piece. There was a Victorian delicacy about it. It was feminine.

"Do you know anything about woodworking? What would it take to finish this?"

"I know more than you do, but I don't have a clue about how to finish something like this. Or how to use these tools. Holy shit, Major, you were right. There was a workshop back here."

If I were going to finish anything, I think I needed to get the workshop cleaned up and in working order.

And to think, I was ready to put a halt to the current project and turn everyone's attention to getting the house in better shape.

No, I still needed to get the house fixed up. I could hire a team to come in and start taking care of that. I didn't have to do it myself, after all. I literally had more money than time now. And I really wasn't Mr. Fix-it, never had been. I was good at telling other people what to do.

22

KENZIE

W ill didn't wait for me to come all the way into his office before he started chewing me out.

"You aren't supposed to play favorites with the customers. I don't care if that was your boyfriend or not."

"That—"

"I'm speaking, Kenzie. That means you stand there and listen."

I fumed, but I kept my mouth shut.

"What do you have to say for yourself?" he asked.

I stared at him and said nothing.

"Well?"

"My turn?" I asked. I was tired of his games, lack of assistance when it was required, and the complete gatekeeping he did to prevent us from reaching out to the owner. If I had a complaint against him, I was supposed to take it directly to him? No way.

Will was supporting, and now contributing, to a hostile work environment. At least I was feeling hostile. I wanted to just quit. I wanted to open my mouth and tell him to go screw himself. But I couldn't do that to Ruby. She needed food, clothes, and a place to live. And it was my job to keep her safe and protected.

I needed this job no matter how much I hated it. I felt stuck. I took a deep breath and hoped I didn't start crying. Maybe crying would make Will feel bad for yelling at me for no reason.

"Mac—"

"How many times do I need to tell you that you have to deal with him on your own?"

"And when I do, you yell at me. He threw away another customer's food because I was carrying it out to him."

"Your boyfriend?"

"No, not my boyfriend. I don't have a boyfriend. I don't even know if I'd call Allan a friend. He's a guy I know.

"I've never seen him here before. How do you know him?"

I huffed out through my nose like an angry bull.

"He works with Ruby. You know, how I know him doesn't have any bearing on any of this. Mac got mad that I was helping Allan out when I won't cater to him. And before you ask another asinine question, Allan has a prosthetic leg. He mentioned his leg was bothering him and asked for help. I think that's a reasonable reason to carry his food out to him. Mac's fit was completely unreasonable. He was acting jealous because I was doing my job. He gets like that every time I talk to any man who isn't obviously with another woman."

I was so angry, my voice grew louder. I was yelling at my boss, and I didn't care anymore.

"Mac is interfering with my ability to do my job. It seems to me that taking care of that little situation should be your job. Now, if you'll excuse me, I have bathrooms to clean."

I stormed out of his office and went directly to the janitor closet. I grabbed the yellow mop cart and slammed my way into the men's room. "Anyone in here? No? Good, I'm cleaning it."

I didn't do a deep clean. The restroom was gross. It always was. I did the bare minimum. I didn't want to be there, and if Will was only going to support me with the bare minimum, I was only going to give back as good as I got.

I slammed the mop cart around, banging on the door and the wall as I rolled it from the men's room into the women's room. I didn't make any grand announcement. I didn't need to. It was empty, which was fine by me. I locked myself in the smaller stall and started to cry.

I hated to cry in the bathroom. But I was less likely to be discovered by a coworker. I occasionally screamed in the deep freezer. It was reasonably soundproof, but it was too cold for crying. And Will might go in there at any time to take inventory or pull more burgers out. He never came into the women's restroom, not even to clean it.

I don't know how long I was in there before I heard Jess's voice. "Kenzie, you in here?"

I wiped my tears and blew my nose. "Yeah. I'm cleaning."

"If that's what you want to call it. There's some guy out here looking for you."

"If it's Mac, I'm not here."

"The old guy? No, this guy is hot."

Tate was here? "Okay, I'll be right out. "

I blew my nose again and let myself out of the stall. My face was blotchy and there was simply no way to hide that I had been crying. I finished washing my hands and then splashed cold water on my face.

I stepped out of the restroom, dragging the mop cart with me.

"Kenzie?" Tate asked as I stepped out. "What's the matter?"

"Let me put this stuff away. I'll be right back." I didn't bother to dump and rinse out the bucket. It would simply be more work for me later.

"Come on." I grabbed Tate's hand and dragged him outside. "I've got a break, and I need to get out of here."

When we got to his truck, he leaned against it and pulled me into his chest and held me in silence for a long while.

"Allan said Mac was making trouble for you. Is that what the tears are all about?"

I nodded. "Will, my manager, keeps telling me to deal with Mac, but when I do, I get in trouble. Allan said his leg hurt, so I was helping him." I told Tate the whole story again. And I included the ass chewing I got from Will. "And I don't have an HR department or any way to complain about Will. I deserve a safe workplace, right? I think Will is going to fire me this time."

"He's not going to fire you. You are his best worker."

"How do you know?" I asked.

"Because I know you, and you have integrity. Of course you're his best worker. Does anyone else actually clean the bathrooms?"

I laughed. Tate had us all figured out already.

"No, just me. Can we talk about something else? Like, why are you here?"

"I came to see you. I'm allowed to do that, right?"

I nodded. "Yes, you're allowed to come see me. I'm glad you did. I'll be able to get through the rest of my shift without breaking down again."

"Would looking forward to something help out?"

I shrugged. "Like what?"

"Let me take you out tonight. A real date. And when it's over, I can either kiss you goodnight or seduce you."

I liked the idea of him seducing me. "How is that going to work? What am I going to do with Ruby?"

"Send her to spend the night at her friend's, or she can stay at my place with Allan."

Something clenched in my guy when he mentioned Allan. I liked him. He seemed like a decent guy, and I knew he wouldn't hurt Ruby, but could I really be sure?

"I'll see if she can spend the night at her friend's."

I spent the rest of my break embracing Tate. It didn't last nearly long enough. And then I had to wait what felt like forever before the end of my shift. I clocked out five minutes early. I didn't want to be there any longer than I had to. I had Latisha put a to-go order together for me.

Ruby was already home when I got there. She had the TV on too loud, again.

"What's for dinner?" she asked as soon as I walked in the door.

I handed her the bag. "Burgers and fries." I pulled the phone out of my purse and handed it over. Tate had me developing the habit of carrying it and checking messages during my breaks.

"Call Heather and see if you can spend the night. I'm going out and don't know how late I'm going to be."

"You're going out? With whom?"

"Who do you think?"

"You're finally going on a date with Tate? Yes!" Her enthusiasm was actually cute. I was glad she liked Tate. I did too.

I took a shower and changed. I didn't have a new dress, but I did have something decent to wear. The important part was that I didn't smell like fry grease. Some days, getting that smell out of my hair felt impossible. I washed my hair twice just to make sure the smell didn't cling to me.

When Tate arrived, I was glad I took the time to clean up. I thought the man was exceptionally handsome, and I had only ever seen him in some form of work pants and flannel shirts or T-shirts. It never occurred to me that he owned a suit, let alone would turn up on my doorstep wearing one. He looked like a high-powered New York lawyer in a suit and a long black wool overcoat.

"I thought you were going on a date. You look like you're dressed for a funeral," Ruby said as she let him in.

"Shut up, Ruby. Tate looks nice." He looked better than nice, but I didn't have the vocabulary at the moment to articulate just how nice he looked. He looked so good, I really wanted to get him out of the suit and naked. He had said he wanted to seduce me. I had no idea all he needed to do to accomplish that was put on a suit and a tie.

"You look nice, too," he said with a soft smile. His glance dipped, and he stared down at my cleavage for a long moment. "Very nice."

He cleared his throat and looked up. "Grab your things, kiddo. We'll drop you off."

"Where are you going?" Ruby asked.

"There's a little place in Shasta I've heard about. I thought we could try that."

The only place I knew of in Shasta that was wear a tie fancy was DiMarco's. I really hoped it wasn't DiMarco's. I couldn't, I just couldn't.

"You can't take Kenzie to DiMarco's," Ruby blurted out, cutting through my thoughts.

"What's wrong with DiMarco's?"

"That's where Mom and Dad had dinner before their accident." I was really glad Ruby was able to tell Tate. She reported it as if it were simply a matter of historical facts.

Words and panic were still wedged in my throat.

"Damn, I'm so sorry. No, we're not going to DiMarco's," Tate said.

23

TATE

F uck, fuck, fuck. I did have reservations at DiMarco's. I knew it was hard to talk about traumatic events, and clearly, their parents' death was very hard on Kenzie. She had barely told me anything. I was going to continue to fuck up unless I learned more. I would have to ask Ruby about it next time I had her out at the workshop. That kid liked to talk.

She prattled on about some video game she was going to play when she got to her friend's house. I barely paid attention, stuck in my head about messing up so epically for our first official date. I stopped the truck where Kenzie told me to. Ruby jumped out, and I waited until she was inside the house before I started pulling out.

"I'm surprised you let her spend the night during the school week," I said.

"Heather's family has been really great ever since... They've taken care of Ruby a few times when I've gotten sick or so overwhelmed I didn't know what to do. Heather's mom is the best."

She rested her hand on my arm. "I know you didn't know about DiMarco's. I appreciate the thought. It's a really high-end place, but I just can't."

"I should have asked," I admitted.

"Not at all. That would have taken away your surprise plans. We could still go into Shasta. They have some great places to eat. They get way more tourists than we do, so they have more restaurants."

"You're okay with us exploring and seeing where we end up?" I chuckled.

"I'd be perfectly happy if you took us through a drive-thru and took me home," she said.

"You want to end this date that badly, huh?"

"Hardly. I want to start your seduction that badly."

I practically swallowed my tongue. "Don't tempt me."

"I thought that was the whole point?" She giggled.

That was the goal. Maybe not the whole point, but damn. "The point was to take you out, show off some more."

"You don't need to show off for me, Tate. I'm already impressed." Her praise went straight to my balls.

Taking her home and getting her naked was now top of my list. But I had promised her dinner. "We could go back to your place and have a late dinner," I suggested.

Kenzie was quiet for a long minute.

I looked over at her. She was biting her lip and blushing fiercely.

"Home it is, then," I announced.

She didn't say anything, just continued to blush like a beacon. She was quiet but held my hand and led me the entire way up to the third floor and her apartment. It took a great deal of self-control not to toss her over my shoulder like a caveman and drag her to bed. Inside, she continued to lead me to her room. She shut her door and clicked the lock.

"No one else is here," I murmured.

"I know, but just in case." Her answer was so quiet, I could hardly hear her.

I helped her off with her coat before taking mine off. I placed them both on the back of the side chair she had. Her room was noticeably tidier than the last time I had been in it. Then again, this time, she had warning that I was going to be in here.

I started to take my suit jacket off.

"No, let me," she said as she stepped in close and smoothed the jacket over my chest. "You look really handsome tonight. Like some movie star. This was obviously tailored for you."

"You say that like you didn't expect me to wear tailored suits."

"I didn't. I mean, you don't expect to see me in designer dresses, do you?"

I shook my head. "Can't say it's something I even thought about. You in pretty things I can slowly remove is what I think about if I manage to get you in clothes inside my head."

I skimmed my hand down her neck and over her shoulder, slowly dragging the fabric of the dress to expose the skin I so desperately wanted access to.

I dipped my head and placed a kiss on the exposed juncture of her neck and shoulder.

She shuddered. "I'm naked in your head?"

"Hmm, hmm," I hummed, too busy with my mouth against her skin to form words.

"Are we doing anything? Or am I just sitting there naked?"

"Do you want me to tell you, or show you?" I asked.

"Show."

With a growl, I swung Kenzie up into my arms. She squeaked and kicked her feet. Her shoes went flying. Good, less work for me.

I set her on the bed and locked my gaze with hers. "Be a good girl and stay put."

I loosened my tie and popped buttons in my rush to open my shirt. Shirt and jacket came off as a unit. I reached behind and pulled my T-shirt off as I kicked the heels of my shoes and finally got them off. With a quick flick, I unfastened my belt and the top fastener of my slacks. I dropped everything at once so that I was before her completely naked. The strip down wasn't for show, but for action.

She climbed to her knees and hummed while she ran her hands over my chest so that my chest hairs laced between her fingers. As she caressed me, I gathered the hem of her dress into my fists, lifting until I could touch her hips and the undergarments she wore. I took as direct an approach with pulling her things off her body as I had with mine.

Kenzie didn't seem to mind and assisted when one of her undergarments got twisted and tightened around her thighs.

I moaned when I had a handful of her skin in my palm. Her nakedness, that's all I really needed, and it was a pleasure to have. I lay her back against the mattress, dress hiked around her waist. I crawled in after her, spreading her thighs wide.

"Tate," she gasped.

"I'm showing you," I said before I scraped my teeth along the soft skin of her inner thigh.

"Tate!"

"That's right, you keep saying my name like that," I commanded.

I had her ass in my hands and her skin under my lips. I nipped and licked my way across her leg until I found heaven.

Kenzie gasped, no words this time. But she managed to grab a fist full of my hair. Good, she was going to need to hold on for this ride. I savored her pussy one lick at a time. Each stroke of my tongue elicited another gasp or moan.

I sucked on her clit until she bucked against my face. I needed more hands. Hands to hold and mold her breasts with, hands to work her hips, and hands to delve into her. The temptation to be inside Kenzie was too strong. I gave up my hold on her ass and drove two fingers into her wet depths.

She wiggled and squealed as I devoured her. My hand pumped into her as her inner muscles began to clench and pulse.

I growled against her, too wrapped up in giving her pleasure to pause and tell her she was doing exactly what I wanted her to do. I wanted her orgasm on my face, and I was about to get what I wanted.

Kenzie rocked harder. She slammed her hand against the mattress, beating it out to the tempo our bodies moved to.

"Tate!" Her voice was high-pitched and desperate. "Oh, God, Tate!"

Her orgasm clamped down hard. Her body grasped at my fingers as I continued to thrust into her. I licked as wave after wave rolled through her body. I wasn't about to give up my pre-dinner treat just because she had an orgasm. There were more of those to be had.

Kenzie whimpered and kept rocking her hips against me. I kept working her, pulling more and more from her.

She settled, and the fist pulling my hair began pushing against me.

"It's so... I can... Tate..." She gasped only partial words as I took pleasure with my mouth against her sex. This wasn't only so she could orgasm first, but because I completely enjoyed it. I was selfish that way.

When her thighs captured my head and pressed together, I relented. Pushing back, I wiped her honey from my chin. Damn, she was perfect and beautiful. Her eyes had that glassy, well-satiated, unable to focus look. Her mouth spread in a sexy grin that I wanted to kiss and claim as my own. Her dress was a tangled mess.

I grabbed her wrist and hauled her into a sitting position.

"That was... wow." She was breathless and limp from my actions.

"Are you ready for more? It's my turn."

She held her arms over her head as I lifted the dress off. She wobbled a bit and then reached behind her to unfasten her bra. Damn, that was a beautiful sight, her breasts all lifted and jutting toward me. Her nipples were erect and reaching out as if begging for my touch.

"I thought that was your turn," she said as she flopped back.

I spread her legs and settled between them, pressing my cock against her slick folds. "Oh, no, sweetheart, that was all for you."

"Showing off again?" She giggled.

"That was just the warmup. Now it's time to show off." I dove for her. She was spread out before me like a feast, and I would never get my fill.

I sucked one already pearled nipple into my mouth, greedy to touch and taste more of her. Her other nipple tickled the palm of my hand as I grabbed and kneaded.

Kenzie locked her ankles around my hips, and that was all the invitation I needed to sink into her. She was slick and wet and so fucking hot. Nothing in this world, I mean nothing, felt as good as her body wrapped around me, around my cock. I never wanted to leave this bed, this position. I would drown in her if she let me.

Driving her to the brink of orgasm again only dragged my happy ass along. There's a bittersweet pleasure in orgasm. Maximum pleasure reached, end of the fun. My body tapped out, and I forgot all about the late-night dinner I promised as she held me and I drifted to sleep.

24

KENZIE

I pulled up the drive to Tate's home. Arriving there after work was a lot different from coming home to the little apartment Ruby and I shared. I frequently pulled into the parking lot at the same time others also got home, but we didn't wave or chat. We all trudged from our cars with our heads down, each in our own little world. Mine was full of exhaustion and depression. I'm sure my neighbors' were as well.

But things were different here.

Allan limped across the yard. He and Tate were still talking. By the time I got out of the car, Allan was on the back porch. He waved at me as he went inside. Tate, leaning on the barn door, waved me over to him.

With a quick glance over his shoulder, he leaned in and kissed me. It was a quick peck, but I liked it. I liked the whole idea of coming home to someone who smiled and kissed me.

"How was work?" Tate asked.

"Work was work. Mac didn't come in, and Will still treats me like I'm an idiot, but nothing's changed. Is Allan okay? He's limping." Allan worked hard to not limp. The average person had no idea he walked on a prosthetic leg.

"He's worn out, headed to bed early. That means you and I are making dinner," Tate said with a heavy exhalation.

He sounded tired. He had a smear of dirt up the side of his face.

"Kenzie, you need to see this!" Ruby bubbled as she came out of the depths of the barn. Grabbing my hand, she pulled me into the dark.

It took a while for my eyes to adjust. I couldn't see where she was taking me, so I had to trust she wasn't leading me into some kind of a prank.

"Look at this place," she declared.

I had to blink a few times to force my eyes to adjust. Ruby came into focus first. She was a mess. I reached out for her hair, to brush some of the cobwebs from it.

"You cut your bangs again," I said as I plucked leaves and debris from her.

"Whatever, look at this." She turned in a circle with her arms spread wide.

"I am. I have no idea what I'm looking at, but I'm looking."

"I think she is more excited about all of this than I am." Tate chuckled.

"Show her!" Ruby urged. She pushed against Tate's back. He barely rocked back and forth with her jostling.

"This is what Ruby is so excited about." Tate strode to the far end of the room.

They had set up rows of LEDs along opposite walls, so the space was well lit. The corners and the walls themselves were still in the dark, but from what I could see were shelves loaded with boxes. There were boxes everywhere. But not cardboard boxes, wood boxes. I guess they would technically be crates. But some of the boxes had legs.

Furniture. "Is this the workshop you thought was underneath all the junk?" I asked as I realized what I was standing in.

"Yes!" Ruby really was excited. "It wasn't under the junk, it was behind it. A secret wall."

"I doubt it was a secret wall." Tate chuckled.

"It totally was a secret wall," Ruby retorted.

I pointed to the boxes that I now realized were workstations. "And these are the worktables?"

"Tool bench, table saw, that one is a lathe under the tarp. It's a genuine workshop. High-end for the time period with all of these power tools."

"But show her!" Ruby was really getting tired of prompting Tate to show me whatever it was she needed him to put on display.

"Fine. You want to stand over there." Tate pointed to the side wall.

I stepped to the side, and he leaned over a bright red and black box that I could tell was modern. It hummed to life. A very not modern set of wheels was next to it with a long piece of, well, it looked like belt webbing. A long piece of belt webbing that went from the old wheels up to more wheels attached to a pole. Tate's gaze followed the webbing up to the ceiling.

I followed his gaze. "Oh, wow."

Dust and dirt, and who knows what else, began raining from the ceiling. Specifically, from the long pole that had started rotating. That explained the crap in Ruby's hair.

The generator did its thing and made the wheels go round, and apparently, that's all it needed to do. Those wheels were the key to the entire system. They drove the belt that turned the shaft in the ceiling.

"All those flywheels," Tate pointed out, "used to have belts attached to them that would then drive the motor on these." He patted on one of the work benches.

"Basic engines," I said.

"What do you know about engines?" Ruby quipped.

"Sewing machines," I answered. "This whole room is like a giant sewing machine. Only instead of punching a needle through fabric, it's designed to turn a lathe or make the table saw do its thing. This is super cool." I understood her enthusiasm. "What are you going to do with it?"

Tate shoved his hands in his pockets and watched the mechanism continue to work.

"I've been thinking about that. I think I want to restore it, and then use it."

"It's a lot of work," I said.

"You're not kidding. All we did today was get this drive up and running," Ruby agreed.

"Yeah, and I am done." Tate leaned over and powered down the generator. "I'll have to figure out a more permanent power supply. Everything needs to be cleaned and greased, but it should work just fine. Come on, we should get cleaned up so we can help with dinner."

Ruby groaned. She would be willing to work for Tate and his amazing workshop. It was cool and new. I understood. Dinner was boring and normal.

I hefted the tote bag I had over my shoulder. "Why don't you finish up before you come inside to clean up? I want to shower and get out of my work clothes before I start dinner."

"Why? You're just going to smell like whatever you cook," Ruby pointed out.

"Yeah, but I'd much rather smell like garlic and onions that fry grease."

"What's for dinner?" she asked as I started to walk out of the workshop.

"Whatever Tate has in his kitchen," I answered.

I had no idea what to expect for food. I was just happy to have remembered to throw a change of clothes into a bag earlier so I could change after work, since I knew I was coming over after work. I had thought Allan was going to cook. The man had skills. But I was okay in the kitchen.

After my shower, I started to poke around and see what Tate and Allan had stocked. Chicken, ground beef, ground pork, zucchini—the fridge had plenty of meat, and enough fresh vegetables to impress me. Canned veggies tended to be cheaper, and I could get them at the Helping Hands Food Closet. But I liked the taste of fresh so much better.

When our situation changed, when I had a better job, I wanted only fresh vegetables. Even if it seemed unrealistic. After all, tomato sauce came in a can. And in jars.

"Ooh," I said out loud as I discovered that Tate had the good spaghetti sauce. I knew what I was making.

I pulled everything out that I would need onto the counters and set up the pots I would need. Even jarred sauce tastes better when it can simmer for a long time, so I started that. I set it to low and tossed in a few extra spices.

I started to chop onion and garlic for the meatballs. I could see Tate and Ruby out in the yard. They were playing frisbee and laughing. She had spent all day here. And she was still having fun. If she hadn't been here, she would have been stuck at home, going out while I wasn't there and probably getting into trouble. She would have been bored and lonely if she couldn't find anyone to hang out with.

The transition from kid to preteen was a hard one. She was officially too old for the school-provided after hours care. That had been the only way I had been able to afford daycare for her while I worked. And now, everyone considered her old enough to take care of herself. She had gone from spending all day with friends to being on her own every afternoon and weekend. I knew it had to suck for her.

How different would everything be if this were our life?

Somehow, the game of frisbee had turned into chase and keep away. I laughed. Tate was letting Ruby win.

Ruby needed Tate almost as much as I did. He was a natural big brother. Hell, he was almost like a father to her. Something she didn't have. I blinked back tears as the unfairness of it all hit me. Ruby deserved parents who loved her and could give her a better life, but she was stuck with an older sister who was struggling with everything.

Ruby crashed into the kitchen first, followed by Tate.

"Why are you crying?" she demanded.

I wiped my face with the back of my hand. "Onions," I said.

With a shrug, she continued to barrel into the living room.

Tate came up to me. He reached out and ran a thumb over my cheek. "What's the matter?"

My heart welled up. He knew it wasn't onions. I shook my head. How did I tell this man that I wanted to be a family with him without making it sound like I was only after his house and what he could emotionally provide for my sister? How did I tell him that I was falling in love with him?

25

TATE

I sat in the truck watching as middle school kids streamed out of
the building.

Ruby opened the door and jumped in. "You again, huh?"

"Who else did you expect?" I asked. Part of the question was sarcasm.
The other part was legitimate curiosity. Who took Ruby to the doctor
and other appointments when Kenzie was at work?

Ruby shrugged. "I thought Kenzie, maybe?"

I pulled a note from my pocket and handed it to Ruby. It was a note
handwritten by Kenzie giving medical decision permission to me for
the afternoon.

She scanned over the note and looked up at me. "You gonna pretend
to be my parent for the day?" A wicked grin crossed her face.

"What are you planning?" I asked.

"Nothing, I promise." She was a terrible liar. "No, this is good. Kenzie
has been a jerk lately."

My eyebrows went up. Kenzie hadn't been a jerk, at least not to me. She did seem stressed, but I figured that was all work related.

We sat stuck in school traffic for a few moments until we were released by the cop directing traffic out front.

"Do you think I'm getting this off today?" She waved her cast around.

"It's been weeks, so maybe." Most bones took a good six weeks to heal. It had been almost that long since she wiped out in front of me. If she was a fast healer, the cast would come off. If not, she'd get a shiny new cast.

"So, how come you can come pick me up?"

"Because your sister is at work, and I'm not," I said.

"Right. So, why aren't you at work?" she asked.

"That's easy. I don't work."

She let out an exasperated sigh. "You're being obtuse."

"Oh, big words."

"Tate!"

I laughed. It was too easy to get her riled up. She was a fun kid to have around.

"I don't work because I'm retired from the Army."

"I know all that. But Allan was saying he couldn't wait until he was cleared to get back to work. He told me you are being super nice and don't even charge him rent, but he knows he can't stay here forever."

I had to think about that for a minute. Allan wasn't exactly physically or mentally fit for a regular job. I was aware of that, but I didn't know whether he was. And while in theory, I knew I wasn't responsible for his injury, as his commanding officer, his injury was my fault. I was just as guilty for Allan's leg as I was for Calvin.

I clenched my teeth and cleared my throat. That was not what Ruby was asking. There was no reason for my thoughts to take off in that direction. Logic knew the truth. That didn't mean my heart did or that I was listening to logic.

"Allan has a place with me for as long as he needs it," I said while successfully stuffing down other concerns.

"That's good, cause I think he's gonna need it. But why don't you?"

"Huh? I wasn't injured."

"Not that, why don't you have to go to work? Allan isn't in the Army anymore either, but he says he has to work. I mean, you've got that house. Don't you have to pay rent, or the payments to own it?"

I shook my head. "Oh, I see what you're asking. If I don't work, where's the money coming from?"

"Yes, that."

I pulled into a parking spot near the medical offices at the hospital.

"Let me try to explain," I started. We climbed out of the truck and headed inside. "If you work for the Army for a certain amount of time and then retire, they pay you money. Like an allowance. It's called a pension."

"Doesn't Allan get a pension too?"

"He gets disability compensation. It's not as much as I get because he got injured after a few years. I served for twenty years. That time difference influences how much they pay you. But I don't have to make payments on the house because I inherited it. That house has been in my family for generations."

"Wait up. I thought you weren't from around here. How can that be your family's home?"

I shook my head. "Not home, house. Here we are." I opened the door to the office and had Ruby tell the nurse at the desk she was here for her appointment.

I continued when she sat next to me. "I grew up in Chicago. When my father died, he left me his properties, including this house."

She nodded. I took that to mean she understood.

"Ruby Hart," a nurse called from the door.

We got up and followed her into an exam room. Ruby jumped up on the table.

"Dad, you can have a seat over here," the nurse said, pointing to a chair in the corner when I took a position leaning against the wall next to Ruby.

"Yeah, Dad, sit down," Ruby said.

I sat and rolled my eyes. This kid, I swear.

Someone came and took Ruby to get her wrist X-rayed. When she came back, I expected that we would be sitting around waiting until the doctor had a chance to look at her films. But instead, a nurse came in about a minute later.

"Doctor wants to know if you want the cast off now or to wait a week?"

"Can I really?"

The nurse looked at me. "What do you say, Dad?"

"Yeah, Dad, can I get the cast off? Mom said you have to make the decisions today." Ruby was overly loud when calling me 'Dad'. I guess she wanted me to hear it. I heard her, all right. 'Dad' had an interesting ring to it. I felt it in my chest.

"It's the doc's call," I said. "If he says your bones are healed enough, then sure. Otherwise, the cast stays on."

164

"I'll be right back," the nurse said as she left.

The doctor came in a moment later. "Another week won't hurt anything."

"Oh, come on, not fair," Ruby complained.

"Leave the cast and I'll buy you a phone. You won't even have to work for it." I blatantly bribed her.

Ruby snatched her arm back from where she had left it held out so the doctor could see it. She cradled her arm against her chest. "Really? I keep the cast for a week, and you'll buy me a phone?"

I nodded.

"I guess I'll see you in another week," the doctor said as he left.

Ruby stared at me and held her wrist close to her chest as I checked her out and got her another appointment. She didn't say anything until we were back in the truck.

"Phones are expensive," she said.

"They can be. I'm not going to buy you the most recent model. You'll have to work to pay for the minutes."

"But phones are expensive." This time, when she spoke, her voice was quiet.

I glanced over at her. She had a puzzled expression on her face. Her lips moved, but she only made muttering sounds, no full words. She tapped her fingers together as if she were mentally counting on them.

"You're seriously getting me a phone?"

"I said I would."

"Tate, how come you can afford to buy me a phone?"

It was a straightforward question. I guess she hadn't figured it out yet. "The same way I can pay you and Allan to help me clean up. Money isn't an issue for me."

She stared at me with the same confused look. "Only rich people say stuff like that. Tate, are you rich?"

"Is that a problem if I am?"

I pulled into the driveway and parked. Ruby was slow to follow me out of the truck.

"If you're rich, and Kenzie is your girlfriend, why don't you give her a phone?"

I had to chuckle. I would shower Kenzie with everything she needed if I thought she would accept it.

"That one is complicated," I answered.

"What do you mean?"

"First of all, I don't know if Kenzie considers me to be her boyfriend, and secondly, your sister is a proud woman. She wouldn't take a phone from me. She wants to prove to the world that she can do it all herself."

Ruby nodded.

"She doesn't have to do it all, but she has to learn that on her own," I pointed out.

Ruby followed me inside.

"You, homework." I pointed toward the dining room. "I'll grab you a drink."

She crossed straight through the kitchen, barely saying hi to Allan. I opened the fridge looking to see if there were any Cokes behind the beers.

"Do you think it would be as easy to cut off my arm as it would be to slice into this roast?"

Allan sounded off. His voice was vacant. It was more of a gut feeling than anything I could nail down, but Allan wasn't mentally in a good place at that moment. And that arm comment shook me.

I looked up slowly.

He held up a bloody knife. It took me a second to realize it wasn't his blood, but the blood from the large piece of meat he was preparing for dinner.

"You okay there?" I reached over and took the knife from his hands.

He sort of went limp. "I'm fine. Tired. Why? I think I want to go to bed." There was just something in his voice, or something missing from it.

"That's a good idea. I'll take care of dinner." I gently led him from the kitchen and followed him up the stairs.

"How about one of your pills?" I went straight to his dresser and found the painkiller that I knew would knock him out the fastest.

He sat on his bed and let me hand him the pill. He washed it down with water from a cup on the bedside table. Allan needed to be away from the knives in the kitchen. Passed out in his bed was good enough for now. But I needed Ruby out of there immediately.

"Ruby, we have to go now. Pack up." I may have barked a little loudly as I raced down the stairs.

26

KENZIE

"Why are you home?" I asked.

Ruby sat on the floor with the TV on too loud. She was supposed to be over at Tate's. I had really hoped to be able to take a quick shower before he dropped her off. He never just pulled up and expected her to jump out of his truck and come upstairs on her own. He always came upstairs with her. Always. I was looking forward to seeing him.

Ruby shrugged. "Tate didn't want me at the house."

"What do you mean?" I thought Tate liked having Ruby around. He had said as much at least once.

"I mean, he said I couldn't be there. He was kind of a dick about it."

"Ruby! Language."

"Fine! He was a total jerk, okay? He yelled at me, and then he drove me home after he promised to buy me a phone if I kept the cast on for another week." She waved her arm up in the air, cast still very present. "When I reminded him about the bribe, because it totally was a bribe, he told me to forget about it. He's a jerk. I could have had my cast off today too."

"He said he would buy you a phone?" That was an expensive bribe. "And you believed him?"

Ruby grunted. She was mad. Maybe now wasn't the best time to get information out of her.

"Let me take a shower and then I'll start dinner," I said.

I had hoped Ruby would have relaxed a bit and been willing to talk to me by the time I had dinner ready. She was possibly worse. She banged dishes and slammed cupboards and drawers while she cleaned the kitchen after we ate.

"Ruby, come on. It can't be that bad," I tried to soothe her nerves.

She slammed her bedroom door. "Leave me alone, already!"

It didn't make sense. She had been disappointed before. My gut twisted. I really hoped she wasn't getting a crush on Tate. He was nice to her, but big brother nice. I really hoped that's not what was going on in her head.

I thought about texting Tate to ask what had happened. But I didn't because I was being very thrifty with the minutes that he had given me. I didn't want to use them all up. I didn't want him to think I was taking advantage of him and his generosity.

I slept fitfully all night long. In the morning, she was still huffing and throwing everything around. She slammed the door on her way out. Her bad mood put me in a bad mood.

"Ruby, I need to know. What made you think Tate was going to buy you a phone?" That had been one of a thousand questions that had kept me up all night.

"Because he said he would buy me a phone if I kept the cast one more week for better healing. I'm not making it up, Kenzie. He said it."

I nodded. "Okay, he said it. But phones aren't cheap. Maybe he has to wait for his money from the Army."

"He's rich, Kenzie."

"I don't think so. I know the truck is new, but that was probably just a gift to himself for retiring. You've seen his house. Does that look like the house of a rich person?"

She was quiet for a moment. "Not now, it doesn't. But that would have been a rich family in that house when it was built, right? And it takes money to fix something like that up. And it's his. He doesn't have to pay rent on it or anything like that."

"How would you know?" I asked.

"Because he told me. He told me he was rich."

"Richer than us. That doesn't take much," I corrected.

"No, Kenzie. Rich. Like serious money rich. He talked like a rich person, saying things like 'money isn't an issue' and 'inherited'. That's rich person talk. That's how they talk on TV."

"If Tate is so rich, then why did he only buy me minutes for my phone and not a whole new phone?" I snapped. I didn't want to believe that he was some kind of rich guy slumming with us.

Ruby looked exhausted as I kept asking her questions.

"He said you wouldn't take one if he had." she sounded quiet, defeated. "Why would you do that? Why would you turn down something like a phone simply because it costs money when he's got money and I know we don't?"

Her words were a punch in the gut. Money was something to toss around if you had it, and it was everything if you didn't. And where those two groups met was a place called control. I never wanted anyone to be able to manipulate and try to control me the way Mac had when he'd so blatantly guided me to mismanage the inheritance money.

I couldn't say anything. I didn't have the words to express to Ruby that if I let someone give me an expensive gift, they would somehow own a part of me. Or at least they might think they did. They might expect me to owe them.

It's what Mac wanted. He promised to take care of us, put a roof over our heads, clothes on our backs, and food in our bellies. I wouldn't have to worry about rent or a job I hated. We could be financially secure, but I would have to be his wife and everything that entailed. Cooking, cleaning, sleeping with him and having his babies.

The thought of him touching me the way Tate had made me want to puke.

She stared at me for the longest time. I couldn't answer her. Couldn't even look at her.

The door slammed shut behind her as she left for school.

When it was my turn to leave, I slammed the door behind me and walked to the car with heavy, tired steps. I tossed my purse onto the passenger seat and tried to start the car. Tried because it wouldn't start.

"No!" I leaned my head against the steering wheel. "Crap."

I tried to get the car to start again. It wheezed and strained. I opened the door. The dome light went on, and it binged at me that the door was open with the key in the ignition. At least the battery was still good.

"Start," I growled. Nothing. That's when I noticed the car was empty. "Crap, crap, crap."

I grabbed my bag and rummaged through it to find my phone. I had to take a deep breath to turn it on. I was still so nervous when it came to using the phone. My minutes were precious. Even though Tate had given me a card to cover the cost of his texts, that covered his texts. At least that's how I budgeted the time. But he had given me that card so long ago, it was about to run out at any moment.

I turned on the phone and checked my minutes. I had five minutes left. Five minutes? I really hoped five minutes would last me the rest of the month. What had happened to all the time that Tate had paid for?

I stared at the phone. Five minutes. I had to be at work in ten minutes, and it was a three-mile walk. I took a deep breath and dialed work. I waited until someone answered the phone.

I blurted out, "This is Kenzie, my phone is about out of minutes. My car is dead. I have to walk to work. I'll be late. Bye."

I ended the call and turned the phone off before they had time to say anything else.

Work was everything it always was, greasy food and gross cleanup jobs. Will wasn't in for half the day, so I was only told I wasn't doing my job right for four hours instead of eight. No one came to see me. Not Mac—that was good. And not Tate.

I was just more tired and more worn out by the time my workday was over, and I had to walk home. I still had to get the plastic gas can out of the trunk and walk to the gas station so I could get enough gas and then drive the car back to the station and put in the ten dollars' worth of gas I could afford.

Someone honked as they drove past. I ignored them. Then I was aware that a red truck was driving slowly on the road next to me.

I thought I would have been happy to see Tate. I was wrong. I just stared at him as the passenger side window lowered.

"I didn't see your car in the lot. I thought you weren't at work earlier," he shouted through the now open window.

"I've been at work all day. I walked."

"Why?"

"No gas, no car." I kept walking.

"You want to get in so I can take you home?"

"Not really," I told him.

"What's wrong, Kenzie?"

"Why did you lie to Ruby like that? You really hurt her feelings. She believed you, did what you asked, and then you just brushed her off."

"What are you talking about? Will you get in?"

I kept walking, and his car rolled next to me slowly.

"The cast. She didn't want it. But you told her you were going to buy her a phone. She thinks you're rich or something, and then you told her to forget about it." Acting like that around a kid wasn't cool. I hated it when people did it to me, but I expected the worst from people. Ruby still had hope in the world.

"I can afford a phone. I didn't lie," he shouted at me from inside the truck.

Maybe I should have climbed in to talk to him, but I didn't want to be too close to him, didn't want to get distracted by him while I was angry with him. I stopped walking and just stared at him. He had money.

"Am I just a charity case for you? Someone you can feel better than because you get to come see me at my job while you don't actually have to work?"

"I don't understand what you're upset about. I like you. If I want to see you during the day, I have to go to where you are since you work. And I don't think of you as some charity case. I can help, so why not let me?"

I shook my head. "No, you're just like Mac, bothering me at work and showing off your money."

The engine roared as he accelerated. Then the tires squealed as he slammed on the brakes before backing up to be next to me again.

"You think I'm like Mac? I'm nothing like Mac. You never wanted to fuck him."

This time, when the truck roared to life, Tate kept driving.

27

TATE

I turned off the truck and slammed the steering wheel. "Fuck!"

I had driven home on autopilot. I didn't have any place else to go, and Kenzie had shut me down.

Who the hell did she think she was to say that what I was doing was charitable? I did it because I liked her and I wanted her to like me. I did it because I could.

It wasn't my fault that Ruby had no patience. I said I would get her a phone, but she had to wait a hot minute while I dealt with Allan. That kid got on my nerves some days.

I slammed out of the truck and stormed into the house, slamming that door behind me too.

"Allan!" I bellowed.

That soldier needed a come to Jesus moment. I was going to lay out exactly what my expectations of him in my house were and get his ass into therapy. He wasn't going to be another statistic, not on my watch.

I banged into the dining room and grabbed Calvin's baseball from next to my laptop. Right, this was the dining room, not an office. I had to get some work done on this house. There was no reason I didn't have a proper office. I shook my head, clearing the unwanted intrusive thought. Right now, I didn't even have time to focus on what was going on with Kenzie, and she was important.

I was concerned that Allan was entering a crisis. I wasn't prepared for what that entailed. I don't think anyone could ever be prepared for a friend hitting a tailspin and going into a mental crisis. But damn it, I was going to do my best. It's the very least I owed him. That's where all of my attention needed to be, not distracted with a house restoration or a relationship with a woman who couldn't admit that I was her boyfriend.

"Allan!"

I shoved my way into the kitchen and froze.

"Officer on deck!" Allan shouted and then jumped to attention. His salute wobbled ever so slightly as he locked down all of his muscles.

"Fuck."

He had shaved his beard. His jawline was dotted with spots of blood where he had nicked himself. And the shaggy hair on his head was gone. He now had a shaved head. But it was poorly done with some spots shaved down to the skin, while other patches of hair stuck up about a quarter of an inch.

He had on the clothes he wore most days, cargo work pants and a flannel over a T-shirt. He hadn't dug out his uniform. I wasn't sure if he had even brought that with him.

"Allan, you…" I was about to tell him he didn't need to salute or stand at attention. He could stand down. But then I saw the firearm on the table right next to his thigh. "Fuck."

I reached out to put my hand on the gun and slide it over to me. Allan clamped his hand over mine. For a skinny guy who had lost so much physical strength during his recovery, he was a strong sonofabitch.

"I can't let you do that, Sir."

I grimaced and released my hold on the gun. He relaxed his hand over mine, and I pulled away from him.

"I'm going to need your side arm, Soldier," I said. I lowered my voice and returned to the barking cadence I used when we were out on a mission. "Hand it over."

"Sir? I need my weapon, Sir." Everything he said was like he was at full attention.

Fuck, fuck, fuck. I couldn't remember whether I was supposed to engage where the soldier was during an episode like this, or was I supposed to try to ease him back into reality?

"Allan?" I asked, lowering my volume, calming my tone.

Nothing. Okay, if he didn't respond to the civilian me, he got Major Bowers.

"Soldier, you were given an order. Hand over your side arm."

He stood there, staring into space, not focused on anything, arm still sharply angled at attention. "Sir, if I do that, Sir, I cannot complete my mission."

"Your mission, Soldier, explain," I barked.

I needed that gun, and I needed it now. His pills were upstairs. If I could knock him out, then what? Who did I take him to? Who did I call? He needed a specialist, not some local rural doctor who would put him on a psychiatric hold for seventy-two hours before sending him out into the world.

At least I had come home to this and not something worse. With the state of Allan's mind, it could have been so much worse. At least this

AVA GRAY

gave me time, time to think, time to act. But I needed that fucking gun.

"To eliminate the competition, Sir."

"Competition?"

"Competition for the lady, Sir. Permission to speak freely, Sir?"

"Granted," I barked. What the hell was he talking about? What lady?

"I can take care of Mac for you, Sir. I know I can. You just need to give me a chance."

My gut clenched and twisted.

"And the lady?" I hesitated to ask, knowing he meant Kenzie. "You have plans for her?"

"No, Sir. She is your lady, Sir. I just want to help you secure her and eliminate that man who bothers her."

Well, fuck. This was definitely bad. Very bad. It had occurred to me that Allan might be a threat to Ruby when she had been here. It's why I rushed to get her home where she would be safe. But that thought had been more about her being in the wrong place at the wrong time. It hadn't occurred to me that Allan would intentionally go after a person.

I held out my hand. "Side arm for inspection."

He moved with sharp, precise action. I was on edge, ready to dive for the floor or across the table if he decided to open fire. He put the weapon in my hand. It was a familiar weight. As I chambered the round, the doorbell rang. I removed the clip and began to disassemble the weapon, ignoring the bell as it rang again. When it rang again, I decided to get rid of whoever it was since they weren't getting the hint, I didn't want to see them. I didn't want to see anyone. But if Allan was a danger, then they needed to leave.

"At ease," I commanded as I slid the gun into the waistband at my back. I would have to figure out where the gun had come from later.

Allan glided into formal at-ease posture.

The doorbell rang again, several times in quick succession.

"Coming!" I barked out. Now was not a good time. I would sign for whatever package and get back to Allan.

"What?" I demanded as I yanked open the door.

Kenzie stood there looking up at me. Her luminous eyes were rimmed with the telltale pink of crying.

"Fuck," I said under my breath.

"Yeah, well I guess I don't want to be here either," she snapped.

I guess that wasn't as far under my breath as I had hoped.

"I was thinking, and we should talk," she started.

"Yeah, we should. Now is not a good time." I couldn't tell if Allan was moving in the kitchen or not.

"I wasted gas to come over here, Tate. You could at least listen to me."

I tilted my head and turned. I thought I heard something in the kitchen. "Shush."

When I turned back to her, her eyes blazed and her lips were pressed. "Did you just shush me?"

"Kenzie, you should go."

Fuck. Her lower lip started to quiver, and tears pooled in those beautiful eyes of hers. I hadn't meant to hurt her, but Allan needed help, and I was the only one around capable of doing so.

I reached out for her. She flinched.

179

Allan's car careened around from the back side of the house. His wheels spun out on the gravel of the drive before he bounced off Kenzie's car. He over-corrected and went off the other side of the pavement before centering back on the drive and speeding away.

"Fuck! You need to get Ruby, go home, and lock the door."

I pulled the door closed behind me as I bolted for my truck. I left Kenzie standing there. I didn't have time to explain. I may have had his gun, but he had been in the kitchen, and it was full of knives. I hadn't secured them. Fuck, I should have secured them the second I returned from taking Ruby home. I had forgotten. Allan had been asleep, and at that point he had no longer been a threat.

The truck tore down the driveway. Kenzie still stood there on the porch.

I should have told her more.

"Fuck, fuck, fuck." Where the hell did Mac live? Would Allan go to the Burger Jeff first? That would be a lot of bad news if he got there before me in the mood he was in. Without a better idea of where to go, I headed there first.

28

KENZIE

What had just happened?

I was at Tate's house to apologize, but instead, it felt like I had walked into a parallel universe. Tate was angry, seriously angry. He scared me. He looked bigger, taller, meaner than I ever thought someone like him could look. I was trying to process his words and actions, and the attitude. Then everything got worse.

Allan came down the driveway like a bat out of hell, side-swiped my car, and kept going.

"My car!"

Completely poleaxed, I stood there like some idiot as everything unfolded around me. Tate growled something and bolted past me. I barely had time to comprehend what he was doing. I was still staring at my car.

It was old, it had a few dings and dents. The paint had oxidized, and the plastic parts were a slightly different color. The light covers were dull. It was an ugly car, but I had never been in an accident, never had the long scratch marks of another car's paint job along the side, or a broken side mirror.

Now, the mirror hung on by sheer willpower.

Tate drove past in a red blur, leaving me on his front porch, his front door still a bit open. Without thinking, I went inside. I was almost back to the kitchen before I realized what I was doing. I didn't belong, and I probably wasn't welcome anymore.

Why had Tate told me to go home and lock the door?

I looked around at his stuff. Sure, the house was old, and some of the furniture was too. Original, probably, but only the wood pieces. The leather couch and overstuffed upholstered side chair were new. The long table used as a TV stand looked like one of those old-fashioned buffet credenzas. But the monstrously large TV on top, definitely new, definitely expensive.

I pushed into the kitchen. The appliances in here were maybe twenty years old. Not new, but they worked. I opened the drawer with the silverware. Old, real silver, not stainless or the cheap, pressed stuff.

Quality old silverware didn't mean anything. It wasn't some identifier that Tate had money. Ruby and I had really good flatware because it's what we got from Mom, and we were not even close to middle-class, forget about rich.

But the furniture in the living room, the electronics, Tate's truck, those all indicated that he did have money. The jerk.

Knowing I shouldn't have been in his house, I left, closing the door behind me. Only to have to face down my poor, damaged car. Reality hit me at that point. I couldn't go any farther. I sat on the steps to the porch, more like collapsed, and cried.

Tate had scared me. Told me to go away. I covered my face and cried. I should never have come here, never should have gone inside and been nosy. Everything about Tate was a mistake.

I pulled myself up. I had to go home and make sure Ruby was safe. Tate's words were clear enough, but I got hung up on the why.

"My car," I whined through my tears as I tried to put the side mirror back upright. It stayed put, balanced for a minute, before toppling and hanging in place. I needed some tape.

My gut clenched. I was now that poor woman with her car taped together. Well, if that's what I was, so be it. I stopped at the Tire Guy on my way home to ask if he had some tape or knew what kind I should get.

"What happened?" the guy who ran the place asked when he saw me pull up.

He was my go-to car guy, always so nice. I felt bad because I didn't know his name, and yet I depended on him.

"I got side-swiped."

"You get the fella's insurance information?"

I shook my head. "He didn't stop."

"You get his license plate? That's a hit and run," he pointed out.

"No, but I might know where he lives."

"If you need me to go with you, he needs to pay to get this fixed."

It hadn't even occurred to me that I should make Allan get my car fixed. Of course that's what normal people did. And if he didn't pay for it, his insurance would. "Thank you. I'll do that. I thought maybe it could be taped together. But I didn't know what kind of tape I should get. I was hoping you could tell me?"

"I've got you," he said and headed back into his shop. He wrapped a good amount of silver duct tape around the mirror, securing it in place.

I opened my mouth to ask how much, and he cut me off. "Don't even think I'm gonna charge you for some tape, missy. You're doing your best to keep this car safe. A little tape is the least I can do for a customer."

"Thank you." I sniffled before throwing my arms around him and hugging him.

"It'll be okay, little girl, it'll be okay." He patted my back before I let him go and wiped my face.

"Sorry, sorry," I said right as I jumped in my car and left. And the more I thought about how some stranger fixed my car and gave me advice, I started bawling. It should have been my dad. But I didn't have a dad. And once upon a time, I thought of Mac as a father figure, but he went and ruined that for me.

Driving and crying are not the best combination. And I had been crying a lot. When I got home, Ruby was safe and sound, watching TV. I mumbled something about taking a shower and went straight into the bathroom, hoping she hadn't noticed I'd been crying.

Even as water ran over me, I couldn't stop the sobs. I swallowed too much water, soap, and snot, and gagged it up. Great, I was crying so hard, I was making myself throw up.

"I feel like shit," I said when I got out.

"Kenzie, language," Ruby chastised me. Fair enough. I didn't let her curse. I shouldn't curse, either.

I made instant ramen and added some chopped-up lunch meat. It was far from fancy, but it was all I felt like I could handle. After dinner, I went to bed. I didn't care that I had a dress to hem for the bridal shop. I wasn't feeling good enough to be productive. Besides, I didn't think tearstains on a dress would be acceptable.

In the morning, I felt worse. My eyes were swollen from all the crying, and my throat hurt. I really didn't want to be a functional adult. I wanted to stay in bed and feel sorry for myself. I had sick time I could use.

I staggered out to the living room to find my purse. Ruby sat at the kitchen table eating cereal. "You don't so good," she said.

"I don't feel so good. I'm going to call in sick."

"Wow, you don't feel good. You never call in."

She was right, I didn't. I didn't want to risk my job. I pulled out the phone and turned it on. I checked the minutes out of habit. Crap. I hadn't had time to buy new minutes since I checked the phone yesterday, and I had only five then. I was down to four.

Four minutes. I could do what I did yesterday, call, tell them what was happening, and hang up.

I waited for someone to pick up so I could talk as fast as possible.

"This is Kenzie I'm sick, I'm not—"

"You haven't arranged to take today off. You're coming in," Will barked.

"I'm sick, and I only have a few minutes before my phone cuts off. I'm not coming in."

"If you want this job to be here the next time you feel like working, you had—"

The phone died. I was out of minutes.

I made my way back to my room and got ready for work. It was going to be another long, tiring day. At least I had gas in the car.

Will wanted to see me as soon as I walked in the door.

"You were an hour late yesterday, and you tried to call out today. Do you even want to work here?"

The truth was no, I did not. But circumstances beyond my control had happened. He needed to understand.

"And then you hung up on me while I was talking to you," he continued.

I hated him and his power over me.

"I ran out of minutes on my phone. I didn't hang up. I don't feel good, and I have sick time."

"You need to make arrangements for that," Will said.

"That makes no sense. I didn't know I was going to wake up feeling like crap. Come on, Will," I whined. I was tired, I didn't want to be there, so yes, I whined.

"Get on the floor and do your job. I only called you back here to let you know I've put you on probation. You need to fix your attitude, get to work on time, and hope the customers stop complaining about you."

"Complaints from Mac shouldn't count."

"With an attitude like that, Kenzie, you might want to start looking for another job."

I wanted to rail against everything he stood for. He was so bad it was like he actively tried to suck as a manager.

I had to run morning breaks. "Are you ready for a break?" I checked with Latisha at the drive-thru window.

The morning rush had finished, so there wasn't too much for me to do. I was supposed to multitask and help with drink orders when the drive-thru got slow, but I took the time to hide from Will and the rest of the world. I cycled through the other registers and was out on the floor wiping down booths when Mac showed up.

My entire body reacted. The hairs on my arms and back of my neck stood on end. I felt the pulse in my neck speed up. A shiver danced down my spine. And I wanted to throw up. I felt trapped.

"Where is your boyfriend today, Kenzie?" he asked.

Instead of denying Tate was my boyfriend, because I had doubts we were even friends anymore, I simply shrugged and admitted I didn't know.

Mac left me alone for a few minutes and ordered something. He sat in the booth next to where I was cleaning. I wanted him to go away.

"Kenzie, get me a refill, will ya, darling?"

I cringed. I hated it when he called me that. I opened my mouth to tell him no, for one millionth time. But Will said I had to deal with him. And I was going to have to clean up the mess, anyway…

I took his cup, filled it and came back.

"Here you go," I said as I poured it over his lap. I tossed the empty cup at his face. "This is not that kind of restaurant. Don't like it? Well, tough."

29

TATE

"Damn it, fuck, fuck, fuck." A constant stream of curse words flowed from my mouth.

I had no idea where Allan would go. I hadn't been into town with him except to the hardware store. He had liked the ability to explore on his own and have a home base to come back to.

Honestly, he didn't go out much. As far as I knew, he enjoyed going to the grocery store because it gave him the challenge of what to cook. I thought he had really found what Colonel Manning would have called 'making his soul happy'.

Only now, after the incident with the knife, and now this, I didn't know what Allan's future held for him. I was damn well going to make sure he had one. For lack of a better idea, I went to the Burger Jeff first, just in case he went in search of Mac.

God, I hoped he wasn't doing that. I pulled the gun out from where it was digging into my back and put it in the console under my elbow. I gave myself a time limit. If I couldn't locate Allan on my own, I would get the police involved and surrender that weapon.

I drove too fast through the small town. Maybe that would be how I found Allan, just listen for sirens and a car chase. I lowered the windows and then laughed at myself. I didn't have a police scanner to listen in on their radio communications, and I sure as hell didn't have any kind of superhero hearing, just the opposite. What was I lowering the windows for? It wasn't as if I would hear anything.

Not seeing Allan's car after circling the lot at the Burger Jeff, I went and cruised through the lot at the grocery store. I checked out the lot for every single grocery store in Flat Rock and in Shasta. I didn't think Allan would have gone to Redding.

Hell, he could have gotten on I-5 and headed to Oregon for all I knew. I needed him to stay where I could find him. I wasn't a praying man. I'd seen too many horrors in my service to believe in the power of prayer, but damn if I wasn't praying to whatever would listen to me. I needed to find Allan first before he could do anything to himself or anyone else.

The sun set and I was still cruising up and down the streets of Flat Rock racking my brain for places I might find him. My deadline for going to the police for assistance was long past. I couldn't take the time to stop and explain everything to them, not when Allan was in crisis and every second counted.

I reviewed every conversation I could remember. Had Allan said he wanted to go anywhere, see anything?

The truck started the incessant chiming that indicated I needed gas.

"Well, fuck me." Allan was leaning against his car staring at the gas pump as I pulled alongside one of the other pumps.

As calmly as I could, even with my heart racing, I strode up to him.

"Soldier?"

"Oh, hi, Major." His confused gaze didn't leave the pump. "My car needs gas, but I don't seem to have any money with me, and this won't work unless I put money in it."

His voice was calm, quiet. He wasn't quite back to reality, but he was no longer in the same place he had been that afternoon.

"Come with me." I took his arm and led him into the convenience store. I parked him in the candy and chips aisle. "Pick out some snacks for a road trip. I'll get your car taken care of."

"Are we going somewhere?" he asked.

"Yeah, Allan, we're going somewhere." I crossed the store and asked the lady at the counter if she was the manager.

"Not me, you need to talk to Marylin. I'll get her for you."

I watched Allan as I waited.

"You needed to see me? What's wrong?" An older lady came out from the back.

"Ma'am, "I started. I pulled out my id and explained who I was. "I desperately need to get my soldier to Sacramento. But his car is at one of your pumps. If I give you the keys and my credit card number, can you get it towed back to my place?"

She looked at my ID that I held out for her and over my shoulder at Allan.

"Is he okay?"

"No, ma'am, he is not. That's why I need to get him to the VA hospital there. They have facilities that can handle his situation."

"Get me his keys, and I'll do you one better. I'll drive it back to your place at no charge. My son was in the service. I understand doing what's necessary to keep those young people healthy when they get home."

I could have hugged her. Instead, I gave her ten bucks to put gas in his car.

"Major, I got snacks," Allan said, walking up with his arms full of chips and candy.

I paid for everything and told Allan to give the lady his keys. He was a little confused, but when I explained she would gas up his car and he was leaving with me, he shrugged and handed over the keys.

I thanked Marylin one more time and led Allan back to the truck. I made sure he was comfortably in the back seat and buckled in. I then locked the console with the gun. I should have done that first, but he didn't know it was there, and I wasn't going to tell him. We were on the road and headed toward Sacramento after I filled the tank.

It was almost midnight before I got to the VA hospital. I pulled into the emergency parking.

"What are we doing here, Major?" Allan asked from the back. He had fallen asleep for most of the drive. "I'm not doing well, am I? I fucked up everything, didn't I?"

"You didn't fuck up anything, Allan. You need some help, more than I'm qualified to give. These people will be able to help you."

He sighed. I went around to his side of the truck and opened the door for him. He hadn't even complained that I had the child safety locks on in the back for him. He carried a bag of chips with him, hugging them like a security blanket. Getting him checked in was not unlike the time I took Ruby into the ER after she broke her wrist. Damn it, I owed that kid a phone and an explanation of what happened.

"You're gonna stay with me?" He sounded scared. He had opened the chips and was eating them meticulously, one chip at a time.

"Of course I am." I reached into my jacket pocket and pulled out the baseball. "I think you need to hold onto this for a while."

"A baseball? Oh, shit, is this Huntington's?" He handed me the chips as he took the ball.

I nodded. "Calvin isn't around to toss that damned ball around anymore. It's up to us to give that ball life. I've held onto it because—"

"Huntington was always tossing this up in the air." Allan huffed a pained laugh. "It was so fucking annoying, you know?"

He examined the ball before giving it a small toss. Once he started, he kept going, watching the ball go up and down. He didn't toss it far up, less than a foot each time. But it did what I had hoped. It gave him something to focus on.

"We go on, we keep tossing the ball because Calvin wasn't given that opportunity. You hear me, Allan? We go on to honor Huntington and the other soldiers like him."

Allan nodded.

"I'm scared," he said after long minutes of tossing the ball up.

"Me too," I admitted.

When they called him back, I stood to follow.

"Sorry, Major, just him. You can't bring that back." The nurse pointed at the ball.

Allan's eyes were wide with uncertainty.

I took the ball from him. "You'll be just fine," I said.

"Will you stay around?"

"He'll be able to come back after a while, just not right now," the nurse said.

"I'm not going anywhere." I had learned my lesson with Ruby. If that person mattered, I stayed put. Allan mattered. I wasn't going to ditch him and run.

The chairs in the waiting room were uncomfortable, but I still managed to fall asleep. The rolled-up bag of chips ended up being a very loud pillow. Dawn lightened the sky when the same nurse woke me up.

"He's situated. He's asleep right now, but I thought you'd want to come back."

I nodded and yawned. "Sedated?" I asked.

She shook her head. "We gave him something to regulate, but he fell asleep on his own. He kept asking about that baseball."

"Will I be able to leave it with him?"

"The doctor hasn't said. Usually, the policy is no. But you can bring it every time you visit."

Allan was asleep. He was in a hospital issue gown, and his leg was gone. I sat with him for a while and dozed a bit.

I woke up when the nurse came back to check on us. "He can't have his leg?"

"Nothing he could harm himself with. We are waiting for orders, but he's going to be put on a seventy-two hour hold while we find him a bed in the facility."

"What about pants?" I asked. The man should be allowed pants, especially if he was being held for three days.

"He can have soft clothes, no drawstrings. He can't have the cargos he came in with."

"If I leave to get him some pants, will I be allowed back in?" I didn't want to be blocked from returning if I left.

"Of course you will. We do insist on breaks for visiting hours, but you will be allowed back in."

I looked over at Allan. He was deeply asleep. I didn't want to go, but he deserved what dignity he could have in this situation.

"Let him know I went to get him something comfortable to wear. I'll be back as soon as I can."

30

KENZIE

"You're going to regret that, girl!" Mac bellowed and arched off the plastic bench.

The only thing I regretted was not dumping a cold drink over him earlier.

Will rushed out to see what the screaming was about because Mac didn't just yell in shock. He went on a tirade.

I stopped Will with a hand to his chest.

"Repeat after me," I said. I couldn't believe how calm I was. I was laughing. "You're fired."

"Kenzie, what did you do?" he demanded. "Wait in my office."

"No, just fire me already. I'm leaving." I took off the baseball cap that was part of the uniform and my name tag and put them in his hands. I pushed through to the employee only area to grab my things. I pulled off the nasty uniform shirt and tossed it on Will's desk. I zipped my coat up and left, only stopping to give Latisha a hug.

"I really enjoyed working with you. If you want, I'd like to do something with you sometime. I don't have nearly enough friends."

"You know it, girl. What's your number?" She pulled out the phone she wasn't supposed to have and handed it to me. "What kind of number is that?" she asked when I handed it back.

The area code was different. "It's a pay as you go phone. I can't afford something fancier. I don't have minutes right now, but I'm gonna buy some on my way home. I'm going to need them to find a new job."

"Hold up, Kenzie. You get SNAP, right?"

I pursed my lips. "Yeah." It wasn't something I went around telling people. But Latisha worked here too. She knew how much we didn't make. She was probably on assistance too.

"Didn't anyone ever tell you, you qualify for a free phone from the same people? You don't have to use that burner phone."

I blinked at her. My jaw hung open. I had no idea. "I... thanks, I had no idea. I guess I'm headed over to the county services office after I go home and put a shirt on."

"What happened to your shirt?"

"I threw it on Will's desk. Look, I need to go. I'll see you later, right?" I could hear Will and Mac yelling.

She grabbed my arm and pushed me toward the back. "Go out the back. You don't need to let them see you."

She was right. I ran. I jumped in my car and sped out of the parking lot. I felt amazing, free. The look on Mac's face had been worth it.

Halfway home, I changed my mind. What the hell had I done? That had been the most irresponsible thing I could have done. I was never going to get another job. Will would make sure to let every fast-food place between here and Redding know that I was a liability.

Panic flooded my system. I couldn't breathe. I wasn't wearing a shirt! I pulled over into the closest parking lot to try and catch my breath. I couldn't focus on what I needed to do. I sat there and panted, trying to get my breathing evened out.

Holy crap, I quit my job. I didn't know if I should laugh or cry. Or both, hysterically.

I needed a new job. I needed a shirt.

My mind was scattered and flailing around. I had nothing that would anchor me to the ground, keep me in place.

I wanted to see Tate. But would he even be willing to talk to me after whatever that was that happened?

I closed my eyes and rested my head back against the seat. I could text him. I didn't have any minutes. I needed minutes. Latisha said I should qualify for a free phone. I should go ask about that. I needed to apply for unemployment. Could I do that in the same office?

I pressed the heels of my palms against my eyes and groaned. There was too much going on. I needed my head emptied so I could focus on one thing at a time.

Step one, I needed to go home and shower off the stink of Burger Jeff and put some clothes on. I focused on that. Home, shower. Home, shower. I didn't want to add anything else into the mix or I would melt from the overwhelm.

I parked and got out of the car at the apartment. Damn it, I should have stopped to get phone minutes.

"No, Kenzie, stop," I said. Great, I was talking aloud to myself. One thing at a time. You drove home, check that off the list. Go upstairs, take a shower, get dressed. The second I started to link about what I needed to do next, I froze up and I could feel the panic grow in my chest.

"Upstairs," I commanded myself.

I trudged up all three flights, made myself take a shower, and changed my clothes. After a hot bowl of ramen, I felt somewhat better. The panic was there, but it had been downgraded to a low buzz and was no longer an overwhelming warning bell. And then it surged up my throat. I ran to the bathroom to throw up. I guess my stomach was more nervous than the rest of me felt.

I needed to get all the thoughts out onto paper. Maybe if they weren't crashing into each other in my head, I could sort them all out. Every single thought and concern I had I write down. Tate… phone… job… Oh, crap, I had a dress that was due back at the bridal shop this afternoon.

Fortunately, it was just a hem. *Just a hem*, I reminded myself as I was still stitching an hour later. The skirt of the dress had several layers, and it was a wide, bell-shaped skirt. I really should have worked on it the night before. If I thought my mind was in crazy shape today, I had been worse yesterday. So much worse.

I zipped through the last few layers of skirt hemming on my little sewing machine. After clipping all the random threads, I wrangled the dress back into its garment bag and hauled it downstairs.

"Oh, good timing. I was hoping you'd be early with this one. They have been calling every hour asking about it," Connie said as I carried the dress into the bridal shop.

"But I'm not late," I said.

"No, you're on time, they're just freaking out," Connie said.

A client started to complain from one of the fitting rooms. "I don't like that one anymore. I need something different."

There was a muttering, and someone said, "Keep your voice down."

Both Connie and I stopped for a second before returning to our conversation.

"You don't happen to have any openings, do you? You know I can work in fitting, or even sales," I asked. I hated to beg, but every few months, I had to ask. I would have much rather worked for Connie than almost any other job I could think of.

"I don't have any part-time openings right now," she said.

"Don't make it tighter!" the yelling client screeched.

I turned as if I would be able to see her, but she was in a dressing room. Nothing to see. When I turned back to Connie, her attention was also on the door to the dressing room.

"Excuse me, I should probably check on them. I'm sorry, Kenzie, I just don't have anything for you right now. Check back next week. I'm sure I'll have more dresses to hem as people start shopping early for prom." She walked around the counter and made her way to the dressing room. She knocked softly and cracked the door open before stepping in.

We were months away from prom season.

Suddenly, the dressing room door burst open and a young woman in a wedding dress, held on with clamps up the back, ran out. She looked panicked with her hand tight over the lower half of her mouth. She frantically looked around before dashing toward a trash can, where she promptly threw up.

My stomach lurched, and I struggled to hold a sympathetic puke down. I swallowed hard, but I didn't leave. I was too pulled into the drama that was unfolding.

An older woman chased out after her. "Mackenzie, what's wrong? Are you sick?"

We had similar names, so somehow, that meant I was obligated to find out what was going on. Connie and the salesclerk who were in the fitting room peered out, eyes wide.

"I'm fine," the bride growled. "The dress is too tight."

"You can lose a few pounds. We can put you in those Spanks, tighten everything up," the woman I thought might be her mother said.

"Gods, no! Don't make anything tighter. It's already so uncomfortable," Bride Makenzie cried.

"Everything is so loose on you right now, dear. It's going to fall off."

The bride ran her hands over her rather thin belly. "We only did it one time. I didn't think I would get pregnant the first time."

"You're pregnant?" her mother yelled.

"Why do you think I keep throwing up? Everything feels too tight, I can't keep sucking it in anymore." With a heavy sigh, she dropped whatever control over her stomach muscles she had been using. The tiniest of baby bumps popped forward. She looked more like she had eaten a big lunch.

The drama was about to go from interesting gossip to something ugly. I took my leave of the shop.

Once outside, I had the urge to heave up my lunch, except I had already thrown that up.

Everything sucked right now, but at least I wasn't pregnant. Right? I wasn't pregnant... or was I?

3 1

TATE

hree weeks later

I texted Kenzie during my stay in Sacramento. The more I thought about how I ran after Allan without giving her an explanation, the worse I felt about it. She deserved to know what was going on.

I couldn't talk to her if she didn't respond. Fine, she could be mad. I'm sure I deserved it. Hell, she could have been out of minutes. If that were the case, I would have to wait until she loaded up her phone.

I hung around Sacramento for a few weeks, rented one of those hotel rooms that came with a real kitchen. I visited Allan every day until they found a place for him in one of their programs. I could only see him on weekends at that point. But I was there, and I took the baseball with me.

"You don't have to come down and see me every week," Allan said when I walked in for this week's visit.

"Come down? You think I'm driving in? I've rented a place in case you need me nearby."

"What the fuck, Tate? You have a life. What does Kenzie think about all of that?"

I shrugged. "I have no idea what she thinks. I haven't spoken to her."

"Did you have a fight? Did you break up? What happened?" Allan asked, his voice laced with worry.

"We had a disagreement. And I think she's mad at me. She won't return any of my text messages."

"No, Tate. No. I can't be the reason you two break up. You have to go back to her."

"You need me around," I responded.

"Yeah, and you need her. Look, man, you got me to the right people. And I will never, ever forget that. I might even come back to Flat Rock and see if that's where I want to settle down. So, you're stuck with me. But I'm where I need to be right now. And if I need you or that baseball, I know how to call. You don't have to, you shouldn't be waiting around for me. You've got a life you need to be living too."

"Are you trying to get rid of me?" I chuckled.

Truth was, I felt the need to be close by to make sure Allan was getting what he needed. My first night in the hotel, I had that black, sucking void of a dream. It felt like maybe I should stick around in case I needed to be there as well.

"You promise you'll let me know if you need anything?"

"Pinky promise, Major. Just don't forget about me while I'm here."

"I'll come back and see you in a month.'

Allan had kicked me out. It was probably best. He needed to find his way back on his own from wherever it was he had gone inside his brain. I packed up the few belongings I had purchased while in Sacramento and checked out of the hotel.

The drive back to Flat Rock felt much longer than the drive down to Sacramento. I'm sure caffeine-fueled anxiety versus bone-tired exhaustion played a big part in that. I drove straight to the house. I hadn't been home since the evening I ran after Allan.

I braced for what kind of damage I was sure to encounter. The front wasn't locked, but it was closed. The front door pushed aside a pile of junk mail and bills the postal delivery person had put through the slot on the door. I expected the house to look like it had been ransacked and the TV stolen. Nothing was out of place. The same dirty dishes were by the sink.

That meant the same food was still in the refrigerator. It would be old and ready to go into the garbage, but it shouldn't be too nasty to deal with. I switched off the lights that had been left on before climbing the stairs to bed. I could clean up in the morning.

The house felt empty without Allan. When he had first shown up, I resented his interruption into my peace. But clearly, he had needed to be here, and maybe I needed him around as well. I spent the morning clearing out his room, washing and storing the clothes he left, setting aside his meds. I even put clean sheets on the bed. If he came back and wanted to stay, there was a place for him.

I didn't feel like playing is-this-still-good roulette with any of the food. I tossed the contents of the fridge, everything, into a thick black garbage bag and took it out to the garbage cans around back. Allan's car was parked next to the garbage. I checked, and the door was unlocked and the keys had been left tucked into the visor. Not ideal, but that woman from the gas station had done me a huge favor. I wasn't going to complain since the car was here and was clearly left alone.

After taking care of all the things that had been neglected during my absence, I cleaned myself up. It was time to face Kenzie. I owed her one hell of an apology. I drove down to the Burger Jeff. I'd learned never to make assumptions when it came to Kenzie. Just because her car wasn't in the lot, didn't mean she wasn't inside. She walked to work frequently, even if the weather was against her, simply because she didn't have much of a choice. Hopefully, I timed my visit properly to coincide with the end of her shift.

Being able to drive her home would give us some privacy. I would apologize to her in front of the world. I would gladly kiss her in front of the world, but she wasn't one for big public displays. At least not that I could figure out just yet.

"Haven't seen you in here for a while," the lady with the long braids said with a smile. "Kenzie leaves and takes all the interesting customers."

"Excuse me? What did you say about Kenzie leaving? I haven't been in town and, well, you know how she is about her precious phone minutes."

"Oh, I know. Did you know that all this time, she didn't know she could get a phone from the state? Poor kid. I'm not gossiping because you know her and know what I'm talking about."

I just nodded. I had no idea the state would provide free phones. I was aware of a program where vets could get one, but since I didn't need a phone I hadn't bothered.

"When did she leave?" I asked.

"Two, maybe three weeks ago. Time just blurs together when I'm working. You know what I'm saying?"

I laughed. "I've been on many shifts like that. What is time when it all blurs together?"

"That's what I'm saying. Can I get you anything, or were you just looking for Kenzie?" she asked.

I had been looking for Kenzie. "I'm here, might as well get a double-bacon cheese, large fries, and a Coke. To go."

I scanned the empty dining area, checking to see if Mac was there. Would he know where Kenzie had gone off to? Should I tell him how close he had come to being a statistic? I had no interest in talking to the man, even if it was for my benefit. He wasn't there.

"Here you go." She held out my to-go bag and cup.

"You don't know where Kenzie is working now, do you?"

"She hasn't told me. I know she wanted something at that bridal shop. Girl needs to learn that they have already decided what she can do for them. They won't ever give her another job, not while she does something they don't want to do themselves."

I nodded. There was truth in her words. "Thanks," I said as I walked out.

"You are allowed to come back and say hi, even if Kenzie isn't here," she teased.

"I'll keep that in mind." I laughed as I walked out to the truck.

I climbed in the truck and pulled the fries out of the bag. Would Kenzie be mad if I showed up at her apartment? What if I started going into every fast-food place in town and asking about her?

Fuck, I was just like Mac, hounding her for a tidbit of attention. I pulled out my phone and texted her again.

I owe you an apology. Can I come by tomorrow? Just tell me what time.

I stared at the message and ate more fries. Maybe this time, she would reply?

After the fries were gone and Kenzie hadn't responded, I put the truck in gear and drove home. I should have gotten Ruby a phone when I promised. She would have texted me back.

The night was long, and even after filling it with a few action movies, I was still alone when I went to bed. Kenzie had only been in that bed once, but I could remember every detail of that time. Especially when

I was just holding her. She was soft and comfortable and made the world bearable.

It took time to fall asleep, and when I had, I wished I had forced myself to stay awake. There was so much trauma everywhere. And the cries, I couldn't block the cries. And then the black. I couldn't breathe, couldn't claw my way out of the void. The black stuck to my skin like I was being shrink-wrapped in it and I couldn't get it off.

I thrashed awake. In my nightmare, I had shredded the sheets and the pillows. My bedroom looked like it had been ripped apart by a beast. I looked down at my hands. Crescent moons of blood were under my nails. My chest burned. That's when I noticed the scratch marks. I had raked deep welts into my skin during my nightmare.

Fuck. What if that had been Kenzie? I could have hurt her, really hurt her had she been in bed with me. Maybe her not texting me back was a good thing. She was safer away from me if I was going to be the kind of guy who did this in my sleep.

32

KENZIE

I stared at the bank statement in my hands. At some point when I was little, Dad had taught me how to balance a checkbook. And then when I was a little bit older, I learned the envelope method of budgeting. After all the misinformation I got from Mac, I managed to cobble together a system of my own. It was halfway between a balanced checkbook, a stack of envelopes, and weekly trips to the bank to ask for a printout of what my account looked like.

It was always depressing, always bleak. But never this bad. I didn't even make it out of the bank before I had to sit down. I didn't have the money to pay rent. That meant I was going to have to use Ruby's money. I was already tapping into her account for our bills.

I had been spending less and less on groceries, relying mostly on the SNAP card. I had stopped eating during the day. I just couldn't afford more than one meal for myself. At least Ruby was getting free lunches at school.

My insides roiled. For someone who didn't eat very much, I was certainly throwing it all back up a lot. And I had that little situation facing me down. I was going to need to see a doctor sooner rather than later. I read as much as I could at the library and made sure I had a bottle of the right vitamins. But would they do either of us any good if I just threw them up again?

"Are you okay?" The bank manager came out and stood in front of me. I must have been scaring off the other customers with my look of shocked terror as I reviewed my lack of balance.

I shook my head. "Not unless you're hiring?" It couldn't hurt to ask.

"I'm sorry, we're not. But you can always fill out an application online, and if you qualify, the system puts your name on a waiting list for when we do have openings." Her smile didn't look particularly sincere.

Had she gotten her job through that online application system? Did anyone get a job, ever, from those online applications? I had spent days at the library doing nothing but putting in applications and taking ridiculous online questionnaires that felt like research papers. One of the applications asked me if I would ever strike a customer. They asked me three different times in a monstrously 120-question long 'quick Q&A'. There was no comments section because I really wanted to point out that one hundred and twenty questions were not quick. There also wasn't a place to say I wouldn't hit someone, but I would pour a drink on them in self-defense.

I folded my bank statement and left. I knew that's why she had come over to talk to me. She was going to tell me to leave. I didn't want to be that person, the one who had to be escorted out of businesses.

"I'm good," I said again as I stood up and dragged myself one step at a time back to the car.

I wondered if I could sell it. Walking was probably better for me, anyway.

I got in behind the wheel and started it up. I caught a glimpse of the pile of dresses in the back seat. It would be next to impossible to take home dresses from Sally's Bridal if I had to walk. Selling the car wasn't going to happen, but I could use it less. That would save on gas for a while.

It took two trips to carry the dresses inside from the car. There weren't that many dresses, only three, but the skirts on them were so big. Nothing for prom yet, but a couple of quinceañera dresses had needed hemming.

I had to wait while Connie helped with a sale. Nothing nearly as dramatic as the pregnancy reveal had happened in a while.

"Thanks for waiting, Kenzie," Connie said as she opened the garment bags and examined the hems. "Perfect, as always."

I handed her the invoice slip. "Do you think you could possibly pay me early this time?"

She shook her head. "I don't run the checks. I send all the paperwork to the other store in Redding. Sally takes care of it there. But I'll put a note on it to ask if she can do a rush."

I didn't want to beg. I didn't want Connie to know how desperate I was for money. Funny, I had no qualms about anyone knowing I was poor. But now that I was desperate, I didn't want anyone to know anything. It was bad enough that I asked about a job every time I came in.

"You don't know if the other store has any openings, do you?"

"I doubt it. Sally has been sending me her overflow. Hold on, I have a couple of hems for you."

The hemming jobs weren't going to cover rent, but they would be enough to cover the utility bill, and that counted for something.

I waited and thanked Connie when she handed me a single dress. "I guess I thought there were more. Oh, well."

I smiled. I didn't feel like jaunty banter. One hem was the difference between having meat and vegetables to put in our ramen or not. At least I could get ramen on my SNAP card for cheap at the dollar store.

I went home. Ruby sat at the kitchen table doing her homework.

"I thought you'd be at the library," I said.

She shrugged. "I didn't feel like it. I was hungry so I made some noodles."

I dropped the dress on the couch. "Oh, really? That was going to be your dinner."

"Seriously? Again? I miss hamburgers and pizza," she whined.

And I missed having the money to pay for luxuries like fast food and take-out. It was so far from luxury, it wasn't even funny. I felt nauseated at the thought of a cheap drive-thru hamburger being a luxury. I clamped my hand over my mouth and ran for the bathroom.

Nothing came up, but it felt like something wanted out. I belched. "Ew, gross." I brushed my teeth before returning to the living room. I picked up the dress and carried it to the hook on my closet door where I always hung the dresses from the bridal shop.

When I stepped back into the kitchen, Ruby was staring at me. "Are you okay?"

I smiled and nodded. Neither were enthusiastic, but they weren't completely fake, either. "Yeah, I'm fine."

"Don't lie to me, Kenzie. You don't have an eating disorder or something, do you?"

I barked out a laugh. "An eating disorder?"

"Yeah, we've been learning about them in health class. And you don't eat anymore, and you throw up all the time like you're sick, but you don't act sick."

"I don't have an eating disorder. I'm stressed, Ruby. It's hard to eat when my insides are all nervous from not having a job."

She looked at me with big, wide eyes. Her hair was sticking up in unruly spikes again. I ran my fingers over her head, mussing her hair more, not that it was noticeable. "You've been cutting your bangs again," I pointed out. "I'm stressed. That's it. And I don't throw up that much."

"Come on, Kenzie. You just ran back there to puke. The stress has you throwing up all the time. I can hear you. When was the last time you had a vegetable?"

I wanted to laugh. Ruby was being the responsible one for once, thank you, middle school health classes.

"We'll get more money at the beginning of next month and I'll be able to stock up on canned veggies then."

"Canned is not fresh," Ruby pointed out. "But we don't even have those. All we have to eat right now is dollar store ramen, not even the good stuff, and canned sausages. You could have at least gotten tuna."

"Tuna costs more than sausages. We'll be okay, Ruby. Dinners are going to be boring and basic for a while, that's all."

"Did my Social Security check come in?" she asked.

"It did, and I put it away."

"Then take some out and use it to buy groceries."

I shook my head. "I can't, sweetie. I've already used it for rent."

"But you always said that was what you spent on treats and…" She trailed off, confused.

"It is what I used to buy us treats, and pay for the electricity, and put gas in the car. You know I'm struggling to find a job. The money I made at Burger Jeff paid for rent and insurance and the phone." I ticked off the items on my fingers. It was a short list. The money didn't go very far.

"I'll think of something. Someone in town has to be hiring."

"Too bad the ski season is over. You could have gotten a job at the slopes."

I sighed. She was right. The local resorts seemed to always have openings for the winter. And the few times that the weather dragged skiing into the late spring, they were desperate for help. Unfortunately, skiing didn't last much past mid-March this year. The only jobs they had right now were for trail guides and other fitness types. I didn't qualify.

"I could go see if Tate—"

"You're not to go see him again. He's not part of our lives anymore."

I knew she had tried to go see him. I had too, but he hadn't been home for weeks. I was pretty sure he left town and wasn't coming back.

33

TATE

The house wasn't that big. At least that's what I kept telling myself in the dark hours of the nights I woke up alone. And I woke up alone every night. The nightmares were worse after I came back from visiting Allan.

I know he said I didn't need to be there every weekend, that he could do this. But after two weeks, I felt the urge to check on him. When I showed up, he took the baseball from me and clutched it for all he was worth.

He was a strong soldier, and he was recovering, would make it to the other side. I had every faith that he would. I left Calvin's baseball behind with Allan when I came home after that visit. But I brought the sucking blackness back with me.

I was beating back the trauma with a lot of sweat and cursing. The first night I could no longer sleep, I stripped the wallpaper from the walls in the bedroom that Ruby had stayed in. Down came decades of stale smoke and dirt. By the time dawn broke, I only had a few small patches that needed a scraper to finish removing the paper.

And with the opening of the workshop, I knew where scrapers were. That first day, I only pulled stuff down. I moved around the house and picked at the places where wallpaper was peeling. I didn't have a plan, only that if I worked myself to the point of exhaustion, I might sleep.

Sleep came easily enough. It was the dreams that were the problems. But the harder I worked, the less I remembered having the nightmares. I still woke up at odd times, but more and more, I couldn't remember what had woken me.

After a couple of days of being randomly destructive, I decided it was time to get a plan. A floorplan. I jumped on the computer and found a cheap program that would help me to 'design my house'. I figured I could take measurements and plug them in, and the program could create a blueprint-style floor plan for me. And then I started taking measurements. I measured everything. Every nook and cranny. I even went up the treacherous stairs into the attic. Between being ancient and smaller than my feet, I had very real concerns that the stairs would collapse or I would simply slip and fall.

I could simply call an architectural firm to come and take measurements of this house. I could. But where was the fun in that? After hours of inputting measurements, I was beginning to wonder where the fun was in what I was doing.

I wanted the house restored, I wanted to be out in the woodworking shop getting all of that old equipment up and running so that I could try my hand at turning a piece of wood. I finished plugging numbers into the program and hit the *Process* button to see if what I input would return any renderings even moderately close to what this place looked like.

"What the fuck?" I laughed as the rendering came back and spun around. I clearly had done something wrong. The house looked as if it sat on top of some kind of bomb shelter bunker. The basement spaces were three times the size they were in reality.

"Yeah, I don't think so," I told myself as I closed the laptop. I pulled out the list I had made for work to do on the house and drew a big X through all of it. Underneath that I wrote, *Call an architect in the morning.*

As Manning would have said, home restoration was not speaking to my soul.

The next time I woke up in the middle of the night, I headed out back into the workshop. I had piles of wood. Some of it, if not all of it, was probably very old, and probably worth something. I didn't know how to easily identify most of it. If there had been any identifying chalk marks or labels, I certainly couldn't find them.

The last thing I wanted to do was throw a valuable piece of mahogany onto the lathe and ruin it. But I wanted to try something. I dug around until I located a four by four of what looked like pine. I hacked off a section about ten inches long and proceeded to fuck it up. There was no other description for the ruin I applied to that piece of wood.

I didn't know what I was doing or what I wanted to accomplish. I was simply playing with tools that were beyond my skill set. But that didn't stop me. I was going to figure this out.

In the morning, when the lack of sleep caught up to me, I shut everything down and trudged into the house. I was in the kitchen before I realized I was covered in flakes and splinters and dust from my exploration with the lathe.

I stripped down, leaving everything in a pile in the kitchen, and headed to the shower before bed. I had more sawdust and wood chips in my hair, and probably in my beard that I couldn't see. I scratched at the fuzzy growth.

I passed out across the blankets with my towel barely hanging on my hips. I woke at some point in the late morning, or maybe it was early afternoon. My schedule was all off-kilter. I trudged back to the bathroom and got a good look at myself. I looked like shit. The fur on my face was patchy and not growing in like some kind of sexy lumber-jack's. It had to go. Too bad I couldn't take care of the dark bags under my eyes with a little shaving cream and a razor.

Nope, that required some lifestyle changes. I wasn't taking as good of care of myself as I should have been. I was eating crap, staying up too late, not sleeping enough. And instead of dealing with my issues, I was hyper-focusing on random projects.

If I wanted to try my hand at some real woodworking, I needed safety gear. I needed coveralls or a shop apron so I wasn't dragging in remnants and scraps of my work. I needed a place to sit, or kick back and think, in the workshop. I got dressed and headed back to my office in the dining room and looked at the list.

Crossing off all the house projects felt right. Under *Call an architect in the morning*, I wrote down, *Learn what the fuck you're doing.* For me, I found the best way to learn was to jump in and get my hands dirty.

I grabbed my keys and headed to the hardware store.

Finding what I needed wasn't too difficult. With leather protective gloves, a few pairs of safety glasses in case I misplaced them, and a thick leather shop apron—I really liked the aesthetic of the apron, a combination of heavy canvas and leather panels with loops for tools along the hip—I headed toward the lumber area. I wanted to ask about a soft wood to practice on and get a yard or two of it.

"Yeah, I'm finally getting married."

I froze when I heard the voice. I was about to turn the corner into the hardware aisle to cut across the store. That was Mac's voice. Even though there was no reason for us to be at odds anymore, as Kenzie and I were no longer whatever it was we had been, I still saw no reason to antagonize the man.

I headed down the power tool aisle, just one over from where he stood talking.

"I almost never thought it would happen, but she convinced me."

He sounded smug. Who the hell would want to convince Mac to marry them? I guess it was true, there's someone out there for every-one. Did Kenzie know? She would be happy to finally have him off her back.

I didn't hang around to hear what else he had to say. I didn't care to involve myself in town gossip. And the tool aisle cut through the store just as easily as the other one. I left the store with my supplies, a few lengths of more pine four by four, and more sandpaper than I thought I would ever use.

With Mac out of the way, I really should try at apologizing to Kenzie. It's not like I had to track her down and find her. I knew where she lived. And afternoons were too quiet without Ruby around. I missed them, missed the way Kenzie would look at me, the way she would kiss me. I missed Ruby and her smart, sarcastic mouth.

What made my soul happy? Having those two in my life.

I couldn't just show up on their doorstep and expect to be welcomed back. I needed to show them how sorry I was. Ruby was easy. I owed her a phone. I wasn't even going to mess around with making her pay for minutes. I would simply add her to my plan. I should have done that from the beginning.

Kenzie needed something special. There was that almost finished piece back in the workshop. It really only needed feet and then a good sanding and polishing. I could turn a set of feet. It wasn't going to be that hard to figure this lathe thing out.

I actually felt good on the drive back home. I hadn't realized that feeling had been missing until it returned.

34

KENZIE

"Where are we going?" Ruby asked for what felt like the millionth time.

I didn't want to tell her. She'd be mad. But I didn't know what else to do. This was a solution, and once she graduated high school, things could change.

I hoped.

"You'll see," I said more calmly than I felt.

When I pulled onto the street, Ruby could see him. He was waiting outside his house, hovering impatiently for our arrival.

"Kenzie, no! You said we would never come back here. You can't be serious." She was yelling everything I felt.

I pulled into the driveway and stopped the car. Mac was opening my car door before I had a chance to say anything to Ruby.

"There they are!"

I flinched.

"Yes, we're here," I admitted.

"Well, come on inside. Ruby, you too, now. Come on in." Mac excitedly bustled us in.

He seemed really different ever since I confessed that I needed his help. He was back to being that kind father figure we had needed when our parents died.

He held the door open for us. "You've been here before. The living room is to your left. Ruby, why don't you have a seat there on the couch?"

Ruby stood, hugging herself. I didn't blame her. Mac's house had a funny smell to it.

"Kenzie, sit. I'll go get us some refreshments. We have a lot to talk about."

He left us alone in the living room.

Ruby spun on me. "What are we doing here, Kenzie?"

"I've been out of work for over a month. I barely had enough money to pay rent. I don't know how I'll be able to pay for rent and food in a couple of weeks. He said he'd take care of us. You'll have your own room."

"I already have my own room," she yelled, throwing her arms wide.

"It's not like you're moving in until after the wedding," Mac said, appearing as if out of nowhere with a tray of glasses and pitcher of lemonade like a little old lady from a TV show.

My stomach dropped. It felt like I was going to throw up. I swallowed hard and forced myself to breathe through my nose.

Ruby went pale.

"Wedding?"

"You didn't tell her, Kenzie?" Mac asked. That tone of resentment and disapproval I heard in his voice for the past several years creeped in around the edges of his fake good-natured mood.

I knew it was fake. Mac wasn't that good of an actor. But I appreciated him for trying. At least for Ruby's sake.

"I haven't had a chance to tell her yet, Mac. I thought you would want to tell her with me," I said.

I couldn't smile as I looked at him. I didn't feel like it. This didn't feel good. I couldn't help being convinced I was making a mistake, committing myself to some kind of prison.

"Isn't Mac's house nice? Do you remember how big the back yard is? We used to come here all the time." I was talking nonsense, trying to sell Ruby on a concept I didn't fully believe in.

"Kenzie, why don't you go into the kitchen and get dinner started? I know how eager you are to make this your home and feel comfortable here," Mac directed. "Ruby and I can chat."

I nodded. I was numb, had been for the past week or more since I approached Mac to help us out. I was desperate, and he had only two stipulations. He'd help. He'd put a roof over our heads and food on our table, but we would live with him. And I'd marry him. I couldn't see another way out.

Ruby was on my heels as I got up to leave the room.

"Don't leave me alone with him."

I grabbed her hand and squeezed. I knew how she felt. This wasn't right.

I should take her right now and leave. We could live in my car. I could stand on a corner with a cardboard sign. There were other options. But I couldn't. I was too tired. I was defeated.

Mac was on his feet. "Fine, we'll all go into the kitchen, if that's what you want."

"Come on," I said gently.

My stomach lurched again when I saw the kitchen. It wasn't even clean.

"I thought you invited us over for dinner?" Ruby said sharply. "So why is Kenzie the one cooking?"

"Because in my house, women cook. As the woman of the house, that will be Kenzie's responsibility," Mac said.

"Woman of the house?" Ruby asked.

With her yelling, and seeing the kitchen like this, I didn't know what to do. I couldn't change my mind now.

"Of course. I thought you were smart. You haven't figured it out yet?" Mac sneered at her.

"Hey, she is smart, don't talk to her like that," I snapped.

Mac turned on me, and then his facial expression changed from a sharp glare to his fake smile.

"Of course, this is all so sudden. And we haven't officially announced anything." He stepped in close to me and wrapped his arm around my shoulder and squeezed uncomfortably tight. "Ruby, you should know that your sister, Kenzie, and I are getting married."

Ruby went pale and started shaking her head.

"You can't. You don't love him," she said. Her lower lip quivered, and tears rimmed her eyes.

I stared at her. Mac gave my shoulder another squeeze. He grimaced at me when I turned my attention to him.

"That'll come in time," he said.

I doubted it. I didn't love him. I could barely tolerate being in his presence. I was doing this for Ruby. "Mac has good insurance, and I'll only have to get a part-time job since I'll have this house to take care of. You'll be able to have sleepovers."

"Now, hold on there, Kenzie. We haven't discussed anything about that. I don't want this place to be party central for all the out-of-control teenagers of Flat Rock."

"Ruby and her friends are hardly out of control." I chuckled, trying to elevate the mood, even just a little.

"You aren't going to want all those kids around once the baby comes—"

"Baby?" Ruby yelled, cutting Mac off.

Mac still had a grip on me, and I couldn't stop him when he placed his hand spread across my stomach and jiggled it. "You're gonna have a little brother or sister," he said.

Niece or nephew. Mac knew Ruby was my sister and I was just her guardian. He wasn't going to be her father or anything like that. He didn't seem to realize or care that the baby I carried wasn't his.

"No, you can't do this to me! I won't let you do this."

Ruby rushed past us and ran out the door.

I turned to run after her, but Mac held me with a vice grip.

"I have to go after her," I complained.

"Let her go. She'll calm down after an hour or two. You and I need to talk."

He was a lot stronger than I ever gave him credit for. He turned me so I was pressed against his chest. I braced with my hands at his shoulders and my arms squished between us. His breath was hot and smelled like his lunch. By 'talk', he clearly didn't mean have a conversation.

I squirmed. I wanted to escape like Ruby had.

Mac's lips came at me like starving, rancid leeches. His lips were thin and slimy looking.

"I'm gonna be sick." I shoved, and he let go. I ran to the sink and turned on the water as I retched up the sparse contents of my stomach.

"Are you still throwing up? How long is that morning sickness supposed to last? I can't say I like it when you do that."

I rinsed out my mouth with cool water and then wiped my lips on the back of my hand. "I don't like it either. I don't know how long it's supposed to last. It's worse when I'm nervous," I told him.

"Don't tell me you're nervous about being with me. You've already gone and gotten yourself pregnant. A little fooling around won't hurt you or the baby," he said.

"A little fooling around is what got me into this position. I think you, of all people, would respect my decision to wait until we're married. I've made one mistake, clearly. Let me start my life with you properly," I said.

I cringed inwardly with every word. Start my life with him? I needed to throw up again. I turned the water on and retched a second time. This time, I found the cardboard tube of sprinkle-on cleaner under the sink and gave it a good scrub-down.

"Do you want a beer or something?" I asked, trying to change the subject, deflecting his attention. "I should start dinner."

I didn't move. I would have to walk past him to get to the refrigerator. I felt safer close to the sink for some reason.

Mac growled and stomped across the kitchen, grabbing me by my upper arms. He shoved his mouth against mine.

I struggled and tried to push against him. But he wouldn't stop, he didn't relent. I pressed my mouth closed, tightly pursing my lips together. I sucked them into my mouth and bit down, using my teeth and jaws like a clamp. His tongue searched and pushed against my face.

I had to get away. This whole thing was a horrible mistake. I couldn't get him to let go. I started kicking. My feet hit his shins, to no avail. Finally, I drew up my knee, hard.

Mac let go of me as air escaped his lungs, and he bent double, cupping his groin. I shoved him out of the way.

"This isn't happening. I made a mistake. I can't do this. I won't do this!" I yelled as I grabbed my purse. I paused to look at him still doubled over in the kitchen. I opened my mouth to say I was sorry, but I wasn't. I wasn't sorry I changed my mind, and I wasn't sorry I defended myself. I ran.

35

TATE

After a long and informative discussion with a local architect who specialized in restorations, I was feeling good. My soul was not fixing up the house. Seeing that the house got repaired was in there, but it wasn't for me to do the work.

Realizing I didn't have to take that stress on felt good. Just like knowing Allan was getting the help he needed because I was able to navigate that process for him. I wasn't the help, but I had been the conduit for him to find proper treatment and care.

Mac was getting married, and Kenzie would be free of him. Maybe now, if she would forgive me, she would be willing to let the world know I was her boyfriend. Or more. I was definitely interested in more. But she had to forgive me first. And in order for her to forgive me, I had to get off my ass and apologize.

I made a quick fry-up for dinner. I reheated some leftover French fries, poured a can of chili over them, and topped it all off with a couple of eggs over easy. I wasn't the cook Allan was, but I could feed myself. After I fed my body, it was time to feed my soul. I cleaned up the few dishes I used before heading out to the workshop.

The lights were on in the barn. At first, I didn't think anything of it. But I hadn't been out to the workshop at all since the early morning hours, and I distinctly remembered turning the lights out. I stood there for a long moment and just admired the long cabinet. The workmanship was stunning, and my freshly-turned legs fit into the design.

I may not have built the piece, but I was finishing it, bringing it to life. As soon as it was done, I would take it to Kenzie as a peace offering. I had been a little too pleased with myself as I watched the lights go off, throwing the furniture into darkness.

I knew those lights should have been off.

"Hello?" I called out.

There was a soft groan coming from inside the workshop. Someone was curled up on the futon couch I had impulsively bought yesterday after dinner. It took half a second to recognize the top of Ruby's head with her choppy hair.

She pushed up into a sitting position and rubbed her eyes. "Tate?"

"Uff!" The air rushed out of my lungs as I was tackled and embraced.

I brushed my hand over her head before wrapping my arms around her and hugging her back. I had missed her.

"Ruby, what's…?" That's when I realized she was crying.

I held on for another minute before shifting so I could look into her face.

"What's wrong, kiddo? Are you okay?"

"I didn't know where to go."

I led her back to the couch. She was such a mighty kid, I had forgotten how small she actually was. The last time I had seen her personality also be small like this was when she had broken her wrist.

"What are you doing in the workshop? Why didn't you come inside?"

She chewed on her lower lip and sniffled. "I didn't know if I'd be welcome. You were mad at me about my wrist, and I…"

I pulled her into a hug. I had messed up with her and her sister. After a minute, I let her go and turned to face her. I let out a heavy breath, uncertain of where or how to start.

"I owe you an explanation and an apology."

"But I…" she started.

I held up my finger to pause her. I wasn't going to go all Army command on her. She was just a kid, and the hard shell she showed people so they couldn't hurt her was full of holes and was quite squishy. I needed to be aware and careful of her feelings.

"You did nothing wrong. I still owe you a phone. I'm sorry about that. Look, Ruby, that afternoon, Allan started to have a crisis. He wasn't safe. I didn't know if you would be safe with him here."

"Is Allan okay?" she asked.

"Allan is going to be great. He's in a place right now that can help him. It's like recovery, but for his mind."

"You're not mad at me?"

"Not at all. I should have explained things better. But when things were happening, I was scared and not exactly certain what I was doing. I focused on getting Allan the help he needed."

"You got scared?" The sarcastic bite was back in her voice.

"I get scared when people I care about are hurt or about to be hurt."

"But you were in the Army."

I nodded. "I was. I was scared then, too. But I trusted the decision makers, and I would stick to the plan and do it anyway. Scared doesn't mean incapable. It just puts me on hyper-alert."

"I'm scared," she admitted.

"How come? Why are you hiding out? Did someone hurt you?" I was ready to go papa bear on anyone who so much as threatened this kid.

"It's Kenzie."

Everything in my body froze. My breath got stuck in my throat, my gut clenched, and the hairs at the back of my neck stood on end.

"What's wrong with Kenzie?" I asked in the calmest voice I could muster. I had to control myself or I would start yelling and shaking.

"She says she is going to marry Mac. You can't let her do that."

I just stared at her. "What the fuck?" I shook my head, realizing I had cursed in front of Ruby. "Wait, what do you mean, she's going to marry Mac?"

"She doesn't even like him. I know she doesn't. She's doing it because we're broke, and she thinks he'll take care of us." She was bawling. "I don't want Mac to take care of us. He's mean and he lies."

Kenzie was going to marry Mac? It wasn't registering fully.

"She could have asked me. Does she hate me that much?"

"She thinks you're mad at her for something."

I closed my eyes and groaned. Leaning back, I covered my eyes. "I yelled at her when Allan was having an episode."

"Like you yelled at me?"

"Exactly like I yelled at you. I messed up. But she could have, you could have come to me and said something."

"I wasn't allowed to. You can't let her marry Mac. She'll listen to you. You like her." Ruby emphasized the 'like'. She recognized Kenzie and I were more than friends. "And she's in love with you. She won't admit it, but she is."

"I won't let Kenzie marry Mac." I pushed to my feet and held out my hand to pull Ruby up.

"Mac says they're going to have a baby. But I know that's not possible."

I stopped and stared at her.

"Say that again."

"Mac says they're going to have a baby. But it's not his baby. Kenzie would have had to have, you know, done it with him. And he's so gross. There is no way she's gonna have his baby."

I cast my gaze from side to side, trying to process Ruby's words.

"Is Kenzie pregnant? Did she say something?"

Ruby shrugged. "She didn't say she wasn't."

I grabbed Ruby's arms and made her look me in the eye.

"Tell me everything they told you. I want every word." I let go of her, not wanting to seem like I was threatening her.

"Kenzie said Mac has insurance, and she won't have to worry about working more than full-time. She pointed out the big back yard we used to play in when our parents were still alive. Mac used to have parties in the summer. Mac was pretending to be nice, but it was fake. When Kenzie wasn't looking, he would make faces and glare at me. He knows I don't like him. I used to be afraid of him when I was little."

I nodded, encouraging her to keep talking. "Come on, let's get in the truck. Where's Kenzie now? You can keep telling me everything as I drive."

"She was still at Mac's house when I ran away. I don't want to live with him. I don't want my sister to think she has to marry him so someone will take care of us. We were taking care of ourselves really well."

"You were taking care of yourselves beautifully." It was a struggle to not growl. Or to run to the truck and slam it into gear. I had no idea where Mac lived.

"You need to tell me where to go," I said as I started the truck.

Ruby continued, only interrupting herself to point when I needed to turn. "Mac said I was going to have a little brother or sister and put his hand on Kenzie, you know how people put hands on baby bellies."

Kenzie was pregnant. Fuck. She had to be terrified, with no job and thinking I didn't want anything to do with her. I let out a long, deep sigh when Ruby pointed to Mac's house and there were no cars in the driveway. Kenzie wasn't there.

That only meant I now needed to find her and tell her she couldn't marry Mac. If anybody was going to take care of her, it would be me because I loved her.

"Where is she?" I asked.

"Maybe she went home."

There was no car in the parking lot, and she wasn't upstairs when I insisted we check.

"Where else can she be? Where does Kenzie go when she needs to be alone to think?"

36

KENZIE

O f course it started to rain. The cloud cover matched my mood and misery. I ignored it. Being wet couldn't make me feel any worse than I already did. I felt so lost and conflicted.

"I convinced myself that marrying Mac was the best thing to do for us, that he would take care of us."

I looked up at the sky, letting the water hit my face before looking back at the marble headstone of my parents' gravesite.

"I hate the man. I know he was your friend, and I know you wanted me to trust him. I should have been able to, but he made me spend all that money in stupid ways. What was I doing trying to keep up rent on that house? I should have downsized immediately and gotten a job. I was stupid then. I'm trying really hard to not be stupid now," I told my parents.

A familiar, deep voice rolled over me. "You aren't stupid, Kenzie."

I froze for a moment before turning around and seeing Tate and Ruby approach. I must have missed the sound of the truck in all the rain.

"What are you doing here?" I asked as I wiped rain and tears from my face.

"We've been looking for you for hours," Ruby said. She started pushing against Tate. "Tell her, tell her."

Tate looked at her and nodded.

"Tell me what?"

"I won't let you marry Mac. Neither of us will." He shoved his hands into his pockets and hunched his shoulders as if that would keep him from getting any wetter than he already was. "Look, Kenzie, I owe you a huge apology, and—"

"He wasn't mad at us, he was scared about Allan," Ruby blurted out.

I looked from her to him, back and forth. "Allan?"

Tate let out a big breath. "Yeah, Allan was in the middle of an episode last time I saw you. I had to go before he hurt himself or anyone else. I should have said something. I let the lack of communication between us go on for too long. I'm sorry, Kenzie. I never wanted to hurt you or scare you. I thought I might be headed down the same path as Allan and convinced myself that you were better off without me. I… I didn't know you were struggling so badly. I never…" He ran his hand back through his hair, pushing it away from his brow before wiping his hand down his face. His gaze moved from me to the headstone.

"Donald and Patricia Hart. I like the heart," he said, talking about the heart designed carved into the marble.

"They were romantics. For the longest time, I hated the name being matched up with the symbol," I confessed.

"Is that why you don't do Valentine's Day?" he asked.

"No, you big dummy, look." Ruby jostled him and pointed to the date on the stone.

"Oh, crap, February fourteenth. I thought you said that was their anniversary?" he asked.

"Anniversary, and the day…" I couldn't say it.

"They were coming back from dinner at DiMarco's when a drunk driver crossed the center line and hit them," Ruby finished for me.

I grabbed her in for a hug. "I thought you had forgotten," I said.

She shook her head. "I haven't forgotten. It hurts you so much, so I don't say anything," she admitted.

"Married on Valentine's Day, hearts in their names, died on their anniversary. Oh, Kenzie, I am so sorry." Tate stood there looking sad.

"Our parents loved each other so much. I don't think either of them would have survived much longer if only one of them that died that night. I used to see what they had as life goals, you know. I wanted that kind of love. Maybe that's why they died. Their love burned their lives short."

"I don't believe that for a second. Some things just happen beyond reason, no matter how well you're prepared," Tate said.

"I wasn't prepared. I was nineteen, and suddenly, I inherited an eight-year-old."

"Hey," Ruby complained.

I pulled her against me again. "I love you, Ruby, and I've been doing the best I can."

"I know. But you can't marry Mac. You don't love him."

"I know you barely remember Mom and Dad, but life sometimes doesn't work out the way you want."

"I won't let you marry Mac. Look, Kenzie, let me help you," Tate repeated, his voice firm. It wasn't an offer, it was a command.

"Why? Why do you want to help us?" I asked.

"Because I'm in love with you. Even if you don't have the same feelings for me, Mac doesn't get to destroy you. And he will. If he gets his hands on your life again, he will squeeze any hope you have left out of you until you don't think you can even breathe anymore."

"Say that again," I demanded because I wasn't sure I had heard him the first time.

"You can't marry Mac," he replied.

I shook my head. "I know I can't. I'm not going to. I kicked him in the balls when he tried to kiss me. I'd rather we live in a shelter than live with him." I let go of Ruby and stepped up to Tate, placing my hand on his chest. "You said you love me?"

He nodded. "I am completely in love with you. I've been refinishing this chest to give you as a make-up gift. And I hired an architect to come fix up the house."

I reached up and touched his cheek, not sure if I saw rain or tears. "I love you too, Tate."

He dragged his thumb across my cheek.

"I made bad choices because I thought that's what you wanted. You are so strong and independent, I was afraid you would reject anything I had to offer until you were ready to accept or ask. Kenzie, you can ask me for anything. Hell, you shouldn't have to ask. I want to give you everything."

I smiled through my tears. "I think you already have. I'm pregnant."

He started laughing, and then I was laughing with him. He picked me up off my feet and swung me around. When he set me down, Ruby crashed into us, and the three of us held on tightly.

After a long, wet moment as the rain continued to beat down on us, Tate stepped away from us. He took a long look at my parents' head-stone and let out a deep breath. "If I'm going to do this, I should at least get this part right. I should probably wait until next Valentine's Day to do this, but I can't wait that long."

He took Ruby's hand and stared down at her. "Ruby, your parents aren't here, so it's up to you. I'm asking for your permission, in their presence, to ask Kenzie to marry me. That means letting me into your family. It won't be me taking Kenzie away from you. You'd become my little sister. We'd become family."

She didn't say anything. Her face twisted up with emotion and she launched at him, giving him the biggest hug. I couldn't hear her, but she was nodding.

"Yeah? Yeah? Good." Tate set her down. He leaned over and asked her something. She whispered in his ear. As he turned to me he and lowered onto one knee.

"Kenzie Grace Hart, you have me completely. Will you marry me?"

I didn't launch myself at him. I was in too much shock. I covered my face and cried even harder. Tate stood and his arms came around me. "Is that a yes? Please tell me that's a yes."

I tried to nod. But I don't know whether he could tell.

"I've got it all figured out. We'll make Valentine's Day mean something for you again. You remember our first date was on February fourteenth? Let's get married on Valentine's Day next year. The baby will be here, and it will be amazing. What do you say?"

He let go of me enough so he could look into my eyes. His were full of questions and doubts.

I don't know why he was doubting anything.

"Yes," I managed to say. Between crying and being overwhelmed, it was hard to talk. Hard to do much more than hold on to him.

"Yes?" he asked.

I nodded. "Yes!" This time, I managed to almost shout.

He leaned in and kissed me. His face was so warm in contrast to the cooler rain. And there was nothing gross or slimy about his lips as they brushed against mine.

When the kiss ended, Ruby was staring at us, her face a contortion of concern, and I'm not sure what the rest of it was.

"If you're pregnant and Tate's the father, that means, ew, you did it? Ew, ew! How am I supposed to look either of you in the face again?"

Tate started to laugh. I wanted to hide with embarrassment.

"You tuck that little piece of knowledge away where you can completely forget about it," he told her.

"I don't know if I can deal with this right now." Ruby shrugged and pulled her shoulders in as if she were cringing away from everything.

Tate just kept laughing.

"Come on, we need to get you both out of the rain," he said as he turned to head back toward the truck.

Ruby ran off ahead of us screeching something about being mortified her friends would know too.

I grabbed Tate's hand and pulled him back to my side. "Just a second. There's something I need to do first."

He looked at me and nodded "Whatever you need, Kenzie."

I turned to the headstone and put my hand on Tate's chest. "Mom, Dad, this is Tate. He's the man I told you about. We're gonna get married. I think you'd like him. We're also going to have a baby. Sorry I didn't tell you about that earlier. I was confused, to say the least."

An obnoxious honking came from the truck.

"Ruby is still a brat. Love you, love you always," I said to my parents' grave before I grabbed Tate's hand and we walked back to the truck.

37

TATE

enzie wasn't moving fast enough, and I needed an excuse to have her in my arms. I bent down and scooped her up as we walked back to the truck.

"Tate! Put me down."

"Never," I told her. "I never want to stop holding you."

"I'm too big—"

"Sweetheart, I am a strong man. I've carried heavier things in my life. You are far from too big. Maybe when you're round with that baby of mine, maybe then. But I doubt it."

"Where are you taking me?" She stopped squirming and held on tightly.

"Home." I wanted her home, with me.

"Are you two going to be gross like this all the time now?" Ruby whined at us from the open truck door.

"Absolutely," I declared.

"Not all the time," Kenzie said at the same time.

"There's a blanket in the back. You can use it like a towel to dry off a bit," I told Ruby as I set Kenzie on her feet.

Kenzie climbed in, and I jogged around to my side and climbed into the truck and out of the rain.

"I want to take you home. We should discuss what you need," I announced.

Kenzie picked up my hand. "I don't need anything but you."

Ruby groaned. "Don't believe her. We need dry clothes, and I was promised dinner, but we all know how that turned out."

I didn't know how that turned out. I turned to look at Kenzie. "What is she talking about?"

Kenzie got very quiet. She looked down at her fingers and didn't talk for the longest time. "We were supposed to have dinner with Mac, but things didn't work out."

"Seriously, Kenzie? Stop being nice about Mac. We got there and he hadn't even started dinner. The kitchen was nasty. He said it was Kenzie's job as the woman to cook. Barf." Trust Ruby not to mince words.

Reaching out, I twisted my fingers with Kenzie's. "You don't have to be nice about someone who hurt you. And being nice to get something out of it is called manipulation. Mac has been manipulating you and harassing you for years."

"But he said he would always be there," Kenzie started.

"Be there to always want something from you, always try to control you," I growled.

"I guess he won," Kenzie said.

"Hardly. Didn't you tell us you kneed him in the groin? Getting kicked in the balls is not something that happens to winners. You figured him out. You stopped the process. You won," I told her.

"Neither of you has eaten?" I asked.

"I'm not really hungry. It's hard to keep food down." Kenzie rubbed her hand over her stomach.

"I've got bread at home. Maybe toast will stay put?"

"I'm starving," Ruby announced. "Can we get drive-thru?"

"Ruby, I don't have the money for that," Kenzie said.

"But I do," I told her.

"We can't just start spending your money, Tate," Kenzie started to complain.

"Stop right there. Yes, you can. I have money to buy Ruby food. I have money to cover your rent, if that's what you want and need. Personally, I want you to move into the house, but you might want to wait until after the construction has finished, and it hasn't even started. I can afford to take care of you. You don't have to worry."

"I don't know how I'll ever be able to repay you."

"Kenzie, you won't have to, not ever. We're getting married, and that's not something you have to do for me to want to take care of you. I won't demand that you pay me back or cancel Ruby's phone if you change your mind."

"I'm getting a phone?" Ruby interrupted.

I let out a sigh. "You already know that. Stop interrupting. Kenzie, the point is, I want to take care of you. I have the means, so please let me."

"Let him," Ruby interjected. "I'm starving."

Kenzie nodded. "Some French fries do sound good."

"Can we get Burger Jeff?" Ruby asked. "I kind of miss the food."

I looked over at Kenzie. She nodded. I drove to the fast-food place.

"Oh, no, we can go someplace else," Kenzie said as I saw the beat-up SUV she was looking at.

"That's Mac's car, isn't it?" I asked.

"I don't want to see him," she said while nodding, confirming it was his car.

"You don't have to. I'll go in. I need to have a little chat with him, anyway."

Kenzie grabbed onto my forearm as I turned the truck off. "Please don't do anything. I don't want to be the cause of any…"

I cupped the side of her face before leaning in to claim her lips in a sweet kiss.

"I will be the judge as to whether you are worth making trouble over. And for the record, you are worth it. I have no plans on getting myself hurt, or even hurting the man. That's his call. I just want to say a few words, get a few things cleared up. But if he starts something, I will finish it."

I didn't give her a chance to say anything else.

"Ruby, what do you want?"

"Nuggets, double order, and fries and a Coke," she answered.

"It's too late for that much caffeine. You can have a Sprite," I told her as I got out of the truck.

"You're not in charge of me yet. You can't tell me what I can and can't have," she shouted at me as I crossed the parking lot in a jog.

I glared at her.

"Be that way. Sprite is fine, I guess," she said just as I opened the door to the Burger Jeff.

I walked directly to the counter and placed my order. I didn't look for Mac. I didn't have to. He was there. The entire time, I waited for Mac to approach me and say something. I didn't think I could be reasonable if I had to start our little conversation.

"She doesn't work here anymore." He was an uncomfortable presence behind my shoulder.

"I am aware of that," I said. A low growl left my throat.

"The girl is going to marry me, so you lost," he said.

I cleared my throat and stepped up to the counter to collect my order.

"That's not what I understand. How are your balls? Did she rupture anything?"

When I turned to look at him, his face was red with rage. "Do you want to step outside with me and settle this once and for all?"

I shook my head. "I don't want to go anywhere with you. But yes, let's take this outside."

I brushed past him and headed to the truck.

Kenzie opened her door and half-climbed out of the truck. I handed her the food. "Stay inside. This won't take long."

"Tate, don't—"

"I'm only going to do what's necessary. You've already injured him. He's limping."

I strode back to Mac, who stopped following about halfway across the parking lot.

"As you can see, Kenzie is with me. She will not be marrying you."

He bristled and huffed.

I took a step closer. I was taller than the man, and I was using that now to my advantage. While he physically hunched his shoulders in a subconscious attempt to hide from the rain, I squared mine. I braced my hands on my hips. As long as they stayed put, everyone would walk away from this interaction.

"Kenzie told me exactly what happened this evening. Be grateful she is as kind-hearted as she is."

"Kind-hearted? That girl is a viper."

"And you are a predator who has been trying and failing at grooming her. You should have been a better friend to her parents. Instead, you just wormed your way in until you thought she had no choice. I am aware that you assaulted her. If you ever come near her again, I will not be content with knowing she dropped your ass to the dirty linoleum in your kitchen. If you so much as see her in the grocery store, you will turn around and leave. If I find out you even breathed her name, when I drop you, you will not be getting back up."

"I'm not standing around here in the rain so you can threaten me," he growled.

I kept my voice even and calm. Keeping my hands firmly on my hips, I leaned in closer, wanting to make sure Mac understood fully my intentions. "Then you can leave. Because *I am* a threat to your well-being."

It took a moment for my words to sink in. His eyes went wide, and it looked like he actually thought about taking a swing at me. And then he sort of deflated and scurried away. I wouldn't say he was all bark and no bite. He just lunged and snapped at people who were smaller, weaker than him.

He climbed in his car and drove off. I stayed in the middle of the parking lot until I was certain he could no longer see me in his rear-view mirror.

"What did you say to him?" Kenzie asked as I climbed back in the truck.

"I told him in no uncertain terms to leave you alone. I guess he didn't like the tone of my voice."

"But you didn't do anything, you just stood there like a freaking superhero," Ruby said.

I laughed. "Not exactly. I got my point across, and that's all that matters."

Kenzie nodded. "I agree. He should have had a cape." She turned and reached over the seat, stealing one of Ruby's fries.

Had they even been listening? Laughing, I started the car. "Let's get you home and out of those wet things."

"We don't have a change of clothes or pajamas," Kenzie pointed out.

I stopped myself from saying she wouldn't need pajamas. Kenzie wouldn't, but... Ruby was in the back seat. She needed pajamas and her schoolbooks. And she would be mortified if I said anything suggestive about Kenzie.

"We can stop at your place, and you can pick up a few things. Ruby can grab her backpack for school tomorrow. I started fixing up that room for you, Ruby. It doesn't smell so musty anymore."

"If we go to your house, where will Kenzie sleep? Does she have a room?" Ruby asked.

"Kenzie will be with me," I said. It wasn't some secret anymore, and Ruby would have to come to terms that Kenzie and I had a relationship.

"Does that mean you're gonna...? Ew, no. I don't want to know. I'm spending the night at Heather's," Ruby announced. "I really don't want to know. Give me your phone. I need to tell her I'm coming over."

38

KENZIE

"**S**ee ya, wouldn't want to be ya!" Ruby couldn't get out of Tate's truck fast enough when he pulled up in front of Heather's house.

She was already in her pajamas, having changed directly into the flannel lounge pants and T-shirt once we got back to the apartment. She had a change of clothes for school the next day and all of her books. Her skateboard was tucked into the pack and sticking up as she ran up the driveway.

I had also changed out my wet things, but I wasn't in pajamas, at least not yet. I did have a small overnight bag packed, and I planned on wearing the same outfit the next day. It's not like anyone except for Tate would see, and I didn't think he would care.

"Are you ready to go home?" he asked.

I liked the sound of that. Home, with him.

"Yeah. I'm tired. Bed sounds good right now."

"Bed sounds great, but I wasn't thinking about sleep," Tate said. His focus was on his driving.

I might have blushed.

"You're cute when you blush," he said.

"You can't see me. You're driving," I complained.

"I can tell by the tone of your voice."

"Hey, I wasn't saying anything."

"No, but you are now. And you have totally proven that I was right, and you are blushing." He laughed at my indignation.

He pulled up the drive and stopped the truck along the side of the house. Getting out of the truck, I couldn't seem to take my eyes off the house. It looked different, somehow.

"What are you thinking?" Tate grabbed my bag from the backseat and wrapped his arm around my shoulder.

"This house needs a family again, doesn't it?" I said, thinking out loud. "With kids and noise and memories."

"I didn't realize how big and empty it was until everyone left. It had a family. It had you and Ruby, and Allan. And then it was just me. I don't really have the words to express what it feels like to know you're going to be here and that we're going to make this our home for our children."

I shifted my gaze from the house to his face. He had been looking at me the whole time.

"I love you, Tate."

He dipped his face to mine. His lips were so warm and soft. I turned so I could hold him and not have my neck twisted. His arms held me close, and I wrapped my arms around his neck. We both deepened the kiss at the same time with parting lips and sliding tongues.

I was lost to him, and it had never felt more exhilarating. He was mine, really and truly mine. I didn't feel like I had to hide what I felt for him from anyone. Not even myself.

He shifted. I noticed, but didn't care. My lips were against his. That's what I was focused on. And then he scooped me up. I didn't protest this time. I kept kissing him.

He broke the kiss, I guess to focus on carrying me up the stairs to the front porch. He struggled to hold me and open the front door.

"You need to put me down? I do have legs," I pointed out.

The door swung open. "Ha, I got it."

He did deposit me onto the first step of the staircase.

"Not going to carry me all the way up?" I asked as I looked up the sweeping curve of the stairs.

Tate shook his head. "I need my stamina for better things tonight."

Before I could sass off and say something sarcastic, he grabbed my hand and practically dashed up the stairs. He threw open his bedroom door and tossed my bag onto the side chair.

"Come here," he said as he dragged me against his chest. "I've missed you so much. I can't apologize enough for—"

I put my fingers over his mouth. "A miscommunication that got out of hand. We won't let that happen again. And that goes for me, too."

"I love you, Kenzie."

This time, when he kissed me, the world completely went away. All that existed were passion and Tate. All that I needed was him. His tongue slid across my lower lip, and I moaned. To have him touch my body again was pure magic.

I pushed on his still-damp clothes, getting his jacket off his shoulders, pulling his shirt out of his waistband. He broke the kiss long enough to kick off his shoes and take off his jeans. He backed me against the bed until my back was against the mattress.

I twined my legs around his as I skimmed my hands over all of his exposed skin. I reveled in the joy and knowledge that I was allowed to touch him, that he wanted me as much as I wanted him.

He eased up on one elbow and placed his hand on my belly.

"Do you know when this happened?"

I shook my head. "I don't. But I can guess. I'm only about six or eight weeks along."

"You think we had an oops on Valentine's Day? I certainly wasn't trying to get you pregnant." His hand caressed over my shirt, and then he lifted the shirt out of the way so he could touch skin.

"I like to think it was Valentine's Day. A little reminder of something wonderful that started that day."

He leaned over and kissed my belly. It was so sweet, and somehow, so extremely sexy.

"Our little Valentine's miracle."

The love I saw in his face filled my heart. It was overwhelming. And it quickly evolved into a deep need to have him touch me, love me, be inside me. I tore at my shirt until it was off.

Tate reached behind me and unfastened my bra. His mouth was wet and warm as he claimed a nipple. His tongue circled it, drawing it to a firm peak of pleasure. His hands held me, massaged me. His grip was firm, and I would probably be covered in little dotted bruises in the morning. Tiny little reminders of his loving.

I cried out as my nerves burst into flames at his touch. His hands were everywhere, kneading, grabbing, touching. He cupped my sex over my pants, and I couldn't stand that there was fabric between his fingers and my pussy.

I squirmed and kicked until he pulled away and grabbed my pants and panties and slid them down my legs and off my body. He kicked off his boxer briefs at that point, and I moaned in gratuitous joy as I could feel all of him.

He returned to loving my breasts with his lips and his tongue, and he stroked me. My hips bucked, demanding more touch. He slid his fingers where I wanted, where I desperately needed him. He stroked and toyed with my folds, circling my clit, dipping into my depths.

And then he nudged my legs farther apart with his knees and adjusted his hips to cradle against me. His cock bumped and teased my clit as he rocked his hips.

"Oh, Tate!" It felt like heaven to have his love and seek his pleasure with my body.

I gripped his shoulders and dragged my fingers down the thick muscles of his arms, my nails leaving red marks.

He pushed up, holding himself above me. He grabbed my leg and hiked it up over his hip, hooking my knee around him. He grabbed a handful of my hip and held me there. His eyes locked with mine.

It was as if I could see into him. I saw his passion and need for me. Or maybe it was my need reflected in his eyes.

I cupped his face and held his gaze as he slid into me. This was perfection, this was home. This was where we belonged, together. I held him like that until he stroked, pulling his cock back and gently easing it in deeper. I dragged his face to mine, claimed his mouth, and fought to capture his tongue.

As Tate thrust deeper and faster, I sucked on his tongue, desperate to pull all of him into me. I whimpered as I tried to gather him closer, not that there was any way for us to be physically closer, but I needed him more.

I gasped for breath, uncertain how to accomplish my goal, uncertain what that goal was. My body was lava, pulsing, throbbing, molten nerves. I wanted to kiss Tate, to bite his shoulder, to scream. I wanted it all and I couldn't have it. I groaned in frustration as I bucked my hips against his.

Tate drove me with a steady rhythm toward the very edge of my desire. And then with hard strokes and determination, he pushed me over the edge. I was simultaneously crashing and flying as wave after wave of glorious orgasm rolled through my body.

I shouted with the joy of it. I wanted this to last forever. I tried to push back, to demand more, but as the orgasm increased, it drained me of my ability to do much at all. And then Tate joined me as he filled me with his heat.

"Oh, damn, that feels so hot," I panted.

Tate grunted but kept thrusting, his beat irregular and jerky, and then he held himself to me and let out a deep, satisfied sigh.

"I'm going to enjoy no condoms for a while." He chuckled.

For a split second, I panicked. "Oh, right. I'm already pregnant. Can't get more pregnant."

He rolled, pulling me against his chest. "We are going to have to make sure when the renovators work on this house, they add some sound-proofing. And we'll take the big bedroom at the end of the hall."

"Why?" I didn't see anything wrong with this room.

"Because, Kenzie, my dear, you are loud when you let go. And we're going to have other people living in this house with us."

"Other people?"

"You've forgotten your sister already?"

I groaned. "Oh, right. I see what you mean. Yeah, it wouldn't be cool to torture her with sounds of us 'doing it'." It would be funny if she got so mortified, but that would just be mean. I thought this was the biggest bedroom, and that's why you moved into it."

"It was the easiest room to clean up. There is a larger master bedroom at the end of the hall. It even has a dressing room. I think that will make a great walk-in closet."

Tate continued to tell me his plans for the house. His voice was soothing, and his arms around me were secure and warm. I drifted to sleep wrapped in his love.

39

EPILOGUE

TATE

Valentine's Day a year later

"Are you ready, Major?" Allan asked.

I adjusted my cravat in the mirror. Kenzie had fussed over me every time I called it a fat, loose tie. So, there I was, using the appropriate term because it made her happy. And making Kenzie happy was the most amazing feeling. Her joy was infectious, and I never wanted to be cured.

I brushed down the front of my tux.

"Ready," I admitted.

Allan wore a similar tux, same dark blue color. Only he wore a normal necktie and no vest. It's what Kenzie wanted. She had a vision for her wedding, and we were here to deliver that dream for her.

"You have the ring?" I asked.

He held up his hand showing me the ring on his pinky finger. It looked silly, the small, delicate gold filigree and diamonds on his thick finger. We stepped out of the small side room into the main part of the chapel. Light filtered in through the stained-glass windows.

The Flat Rock chapel was small and full of flowers, not ours, but for a wedding in the early evening. I should have known Valentine's Day weddings were a big deal, and Flat Rock, being a ski town, was considered a destination wedding location.

It was ten in the morning, and we were scheduled for the first wedding of the day. I was under the impression that on days like this one, it was as if there were a revolving door into the chapel, and they ran weddings every other hour.

Early worked for us. We weren't having a large wedding, just a few friends. The baby should be awake for the ceremony and then go down for her first nap of the day when we headed out to our celebration brunch.

I stood next to the preacher. Allan stood next to me. I waited for a few moments before the music started. When I turned, I saw my baby girl. Ruby wore Paris in a front-carrying pack. She kicked her feet when she saw me, and even Ruby was smiling.

I hadn't been allowed to see Kenzie's dress. She had taken over one of the downstairs rooms immediately after the reconstruction crew finished and turned it into her sewing workroom, and then she banned me from entering. All I knew was there was a lot of fabric involved.

When Kenzie stepped into the chapel… my heart skipped a beat. She was perfect.

"Steady there," Allan said, putting his hand on my shoulder.

Her dress was a froth of pink and cream, and while it was very much a wedding dress, it was somehow more. She looked like an angel. It wasn't until later that I noticed that she had incorporated into the patterning of the skirt her parents' silhouettes in large lace hearts. It seemed fitting to have them with us that way.

The ceremony passed as a rush of noise in my ears. I followed the instructions, repeated the words I was told to repeat, said 'I will' when asked. Allan handed me the ring, and I placed it on Kenzie's finger when told to do so.

I had always thought the instructions during wedding ceremonies were overkill. Everyone knew what to do and when. I hadn't realized they were necessary until I forgot everything I knew. If the preacher had asked me to say my name, I would have looked at him with confusion. I had a name. What was a name?

All I knew at that point was that Kenzie was beautiful, and I was the luckiest man in the world. Beyond that, I didn't know what I was doing. Without guidance, I would have stood there holding her hand, staring into her big, luminous eyes, smiling like an idiot.

I even had to be told I could kiss her and that this was our first kiss as husband and wife.

The noise in my ears turned to the applause of our friends as the kiss ended. We started to walk down the aisle, only to have Paris start to cry.

"Mommy's not leaving," she said as she took her hand out of mine and picked Paris up out of Ruby's charge.

Latisha swooped in with a large scarf. "Here, cover your dress. You don't want that baby girl spitting up on you."

Our celebratory exit became a huddle of everyone gathered around us and the baby.

"She's tired," Kenzie said, gently rocking her. "And this is a bit overwhelming."

I had one arm around Kenzie's back and cleared the path with the other as we resumed our promenade out of the chapel. In the vestibule, I wrapped Kenzie in a thick cloak that was more like a red velvet blanket rimmed with white fur. I shrugged into my overcoat as everyone around us all pulled on their coats.

It was too cold to simply run from the building into the waiting limo. But once properly wrapped up, we headed outside where our friends pelted us with bird seed. Well, Ruby, specifically. Everyone else tossed the seeds into the air to rain gently down on us. Ruby threw her hand full of seed directly at me.

The waiting limo did not whisk us away. It took a few moments to get Paris settled into her car seat. Only then was the driver allowed to move.

Kenzie lay against my chest as I pulled her into my arms.

"Good morning, wife," I said right before I kissed her. She tasted like strawberries.

"What a morning. It's been crazy, nonstop, and look at us, we're married." She sounded shocked.

"It's fabulous, isn't it?" I chuckled.

"I think so, but my head is spinning and I'm suddenly exhausted. Did I remember to say, 'I do'?"

"I'm pretty sure you did. I had to be told what to say. Thank you for not insisting that we write our own vows."

"I made my own dress. I think that was plenty for me to do."

"And it is a beautiful dress," I crooned as I stroked her soft cheek.

"You didn't even look at it. What color is it?" she demanded.

"Pink and white," I answered.

"it's cream," she corrected.

"Cream is white," I replied. "You look beautiful. Cream or white, you look good enough to eat." I went to kiss her again, but Paris decided that we were done flirting and she needed attention.

"Did you bring the diaper bag? Are we almost at the restaurant?"

I lifted the diaper bag from the side seat and handed it over. "We're almost there."

"Let the driver know I'm going to feed and change Paris when we get there, so he should pull over somewhere out of the way."

I passed her instructions along to the driver. Once stopped, Kenzie took Paris out of her car seat, and I prepped a bottle for her. As Kenzie held Paris to feed her, someone knocked on the limo's window.

"What?" I asked as I lowered the window.

Ruby stood there making faces at us. "Everyone is wondering why you aren't coming inside. They're being gross saying you're doing it in the car."

"We aren't doing it." I laughed. "Your sister is feeding Paris. We'll change her, and then we'll be inside."

"I can change her," Ruby volunteered.

"She's almost asleep. We'll be there in a few minutes."

"Okay," Ruby said with a shrug before turning around. "You owe me ten dollars," I heard her say to someone as she walked away, and I raised the window.

Paris fell asleep just before she finished the bottle. I got her into a fresh diaper, something that I was learning was easier while she was asleep because she wanted to kick too much when awake.

Kenzie climbed out of the limo holding the sleeping baby while I unfastened the car seat that would serve as a bassinet with a handle I could carry while she slept.

Our party was tucked into the back party room of the restaurant, and everyone applauded at our arrival. It wasn't a large party. We had a few tables, and everyone was served mimosas for the toasts. The cake was more a tower of cinnamon roll decadence than a proper cake. It was delicious.

After the cake was served and toasts were given, Ruby stood up and picked up the microphone.

"Hi, it's me again." She waved awkwardly at our guests. "We don't have a band or a DJ, so we have a boombox" She gestured toward a vintage-style tape deck that Allan set up on the corner of a table.

"As you know, Mom and Dad can't be here with us. But they would have wanted to. I know Kenzie doesn't think I remember them very well. But I do. And I remember their favorite song. Every time this song came on a playlist, or one of those mix CDs they would put together, they would say it was their favorite. It was their wedding song, the one they danced to."

As Ruby talked, Kenzie grabbed my hand and squeezed. I felt emotions lodge in my throat at the tribute, and when I looked at my wife, she was quietly crying.

"I know you didn't plan on having a first dance, so Allan helped me to make sure you got to dance to this." Ruby pressed *Play*.

I didn't recognize the song immediately, but Kenzie did, and a sob shook her. I was going to tell her she didn't need to dance if she was going to be upset by it, but she dragged me out to the small area of cleared floor by the cake table and clutched me as we swayed to her parents' favorite song by Peter Gabriel.

I tipped up Kenzie's face so I could look at her. I wiped her tears away with my thumb.

The lyrics were perfect. *In your eyes, I am complete.* In my eyes, she was.

40

EXCERPT: CHARMED BY THE MAFIA

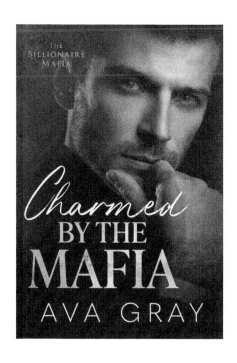

O nly a billionaire mafia could think he could escape death.

I'm his heart specialist, and he's the patient I absolutely can't resist.

So, when he called me his girlfriend to please his family, I could only nod in agreement.

Giovanni might be my forbidden patient and fake lover...

But I have real dreams about him taking my V-card.

Soon, these dreams would turn into nightmares.

His life is filled with danger.

And mine feels heavier now that I'm carrying the burden of his secrets.

Giovanni only has a few months left to live if we fail at treating him.

But I may not even have that much time remaining.

Giovanni will have to find a way to save my life from his own people.

Especially now that I'm carrying the child, he'd never want to lose...

Giovanni

Something isn't right.

The thought filters through my head as I struggle to pull in a breath. I'm halfway up the stairs and it feels like my heart is going to explode right out of my chest. After swiping a hand across my sweaty brow, I lay my palm against the wall above the railing and try not to panic.

For several moments, I don't move and just listen to the rapid drumming in my ears. Yeah, something is definitely wrong with me, and I have a feeling it's not good.

Lately, any little thing I do takes a herculean effort. And it's beginning to worry me. However, I've been doing my best to ignore the odd symptoms popping up. Like how my thirty-one-year-old ass can't walk up a flight of steps without getting winded. Or, how I'm always tired all the time no matter how much sleep I get. Which, of course, only makes me more grumpy than usual.

I keep telling myself I'm young and it's nothing serious. No need to worry. There's also the ridiculous amount of stress I'm under, too, and that would be enough to make anyone not feel well. My father is looking to me to take over the family business so he can retire soon. Matteo Marino knows how to apply the pressure and pour on the guilt to get his way.

Maybe any other eldest son would be excited and chomping at the bit to take over a billion-dollar empire. My father has certainly prepared me for it. But, lately, the honest to God truth is I don't want it. Any of it. Not the multi-million-dollar corporations, not the shady under-ground dealings and certainly not the weight of his legacy. It's suffocating.

Which probably wouldn't make sense to most people. But do I really want to be remembered like he will be? As a ruthless man who would choose money over his own family? A father who disinherited his daughters because they married rivals? A grandfather who chose not to meet his grandchildren because he couldn't come to terms with the fact that his daughters fell in love with men from the O'Shea family? Same with his son. My younger brother Luca recently wed Finley O'Shea. And what started out as a contract eventually turned into something real and beautiful.

The reality is my father's billion-dollar empire was built on selfish decisions, eliminating rivals and dirty dealings. The whole thing makes me a little sick. But he keeps looking at me, expecting me to be excited about stepping into his shoes. And I'm not. I haven't been feeling well for weeks now and, even though I'm trying not to worry about my deteriorating health, I can't help it. The symptoms are getting to be too much to ignore. Though I'm still trying my damndest to pretend like I'm healthy as a horse.

Even though I can't walk up a goddamn flight of stairs.

This is ridiculous, Gio. Get your shit together. You're fine.

I lay a hand on my chest and feel the rapid, out of control beating of my heart. Squeezing my eyes shut, I stand there and wait until it slows down and I'm breathing more normally again. Then I open my eyes again, look up the steps and realize I have about ten more to go.

But it may as well be one thousand. *Fuck.* I drop down on a step and rake my fingers through my thick, dark hair. What is wrong with me? Trying not to panic, I spend the next few minutes convincing myself I'm just under a lot of stress. Maybe I'm having a panic attack. I'll go to bed earlier tonight. Lay off the whiskey. Start taking my vitamins again. Everything will be fine and go back to normal.

Or, at least, that's what I try to convince myself.

"Get up, Gio," I growl under my breath. Reaching for the hand railing, I gather up my strength, and pull, heaving myself back up onto my feet. It takes some effort, but I stand up and nod. Okay, I did it. We're good to go.

I force myself to walk up the rest of the steps and, by the time I reach my bedroom, I'm ready to pass out from exhaustion. Dropping down onto my bed, I sprawl out on my back, a hand falling on my chest, and gaze up at the ceiling. I just need a quick nap. Then everything will be better after I'm refreshed and rested. My head turns to look at the clock on my nightstand. It's only eleven in the morning and I got up two hours ago. Yet, my body feels like it's been going nonstop for hours already. Days even.

Yeah, something is definitely not right, but I'll feel better after a nap. Twenty minutes ought to do the trick, I think, as I doze off.

Five hours later, the ringing of my phone wakes me up and I'm shocked to see how long I slept. I grab my phone, swipe the bar over, and try not to yawn, as I answer.

"Hey, Luca."

"Gio! I'm running late, but I'll be there in twenty minutes."

Late? For what? Pushing myself up onto my elbow, I frown.

"Sorry, but Finley and I were—" His voice trails off.

Yeah, I can pretty much guess what my younger brother and his pretty wife were doing. They're still newlyweds and even though the whole thing started out as an arranged marriage and they signed a contract with the intention of getting it annulled after three months, they fell in love. Hard and fast. Just another twisted thing my father set up to help himself. Although, he told all of us he regretted disinheriting Rory and Sofia and wanted to make up for it by fully supporting Luca and Finley O'Shea's marriage...of convenience.

But, once again, he was only lying to benefit himself.

"Yeah, I get it," I tell him, smothering a chuckle. "I'm, ah, actually running a little behind myself."

"Do you want to reschedule?"

"Nah, it's fine. I'll see you twenty."

"Okay, see you soon!"

After hanging up, it occurs to me yet again that Matteo Marino's ulterior motives always root back to his desire for more power and more money. As if the selfish bastard didn't have enough. He never cared about mending relations between our family and the O'Shea family like he claimed. He merely wanted to rally and build up support from his friends and business associates so they would turn on Desmond O'Shea who had taken over his family's business dealings.

But, after a war with Desmond, the O'Shea's triumphed, regained control of their compound and empire, and now Desmond is dead.

My father managed to put on a good show for a while and we all thought he turned over a new leaf. Yeah, right. Eventually, his true colors showed, and Luca told us he wasn't willing to trade Sean Flannigan, his captive, to save Finley's life. Flannigan was a pawn in his game and one he refused to give up. Even if it meant letting the woman Luca loved die.

Of course, Luca didn't allow it to happen, and he and the O'Shea brothers rescued Finley from Desmond's clutches. After a showdown on the upper level of their compound, Desmond somehow plummeted to his death. Finley was the only one with him when it happened, and it boggles my brain to think that tiny redhead managed to kill her evil uncle. I don't know all of the details, but, somehow, she took care of him, and it was a good thing.

Now, though, everyone is mad at my father again because he handed Finley over to the wolves. After escaping, she told us Desmond said he'd hired an assassin to take Matteo out. We aren't sure if that's true or not, but my father hasn't been leaving the house and I'm pretty sure he's beefed up the security. So, I'm going to assume he's worried about Desmond's threat. And I wouldn't put it past the man. He was out for everyone's blood, mostly his own family's, but he and my father hated each other.

Pushing thoughts of my father aside, I sit up, slide my legs off the bed and pause before standing up. Then I pull in a deep breath and stand up to my full height. Okay, so far, so good. No dizziness or exhaustion. Yet.

But I still have to change, drive over to the tennis courts and play a physical game against my very athletic, younger brother. I have a pretty good feeling that I'm going to suggest we end the game early and go down to the bar to get a drink instead.

Once I'm wearing sweatshirt and sweatpants, I grab my racket and coat and head downstairs. Even though it's a nice day, it's still the end of November in Chicago and that could mean anything. Sun one minute, rain the next.

Going down is easier than coming up, so I'm feeling pretty good. I head outside, jog down the steps of the brownstone—I never realized how many goddamn steps this place has until they started taking their toll—and slip into my Porsche Panamera parked at the curb. It's a super luxurious car while also being sporty and perfect for me because I enjoy having the best of both worlds.

The tennis courts aren't far away and, by the time I get there, get out and walk onto the court, I'm still feeling good. Relief washes through me. All I needed was a nap. Nothing to worry over.

Luca isn't here yet, so I gratefully drop onto a bench and set my racket down. Even though I'm feeling okay at the moment, I don't want to over-exert myself. Luca is competitive and so am I, so neither of us takes it easy on the other. We both like to win.

Draping an arm along the back of the bench, I look up at the trees. The few leaves that are left on the trees are barely hanging on, fluttering in the breeze. Just a few weeks ago, they were all different colors, so vibrant and pretty. I love the seasons and how the leaves change from green to orange, gold and red. I've never minded the cold weather and right now it feels invigorating. Refreshing and crisp as it fills my lungs, expanding them.

Slipping my coat off, feeling a little warm, I realize it's going to be December soon and then Christmas in the blink of an eye. The holidays seem to sneak up faster and faster every year. Things are so different now that my siblings are all married. Rory and Liam have a son named Griffin who is a year and a half, while Sofia and Rafferty have Killian. Luca and Finley just found out they're pregnant and I'll have a new nephew or niece next June. It's a little mind-boggling.

I'm happy for them and the love they've found. But the truth is I've been feeling a little lost. And a lot out of the loop lately. Now that my sisters and brother have found their significant others, I don't see them as much. They're busy with their families and I get that. My mom also moved out of the brownstone not long ago and is living over at the O'Shea compound. It seems that just about everyone has left. They've had enough of Matteo Marino and all of the hurt he's caused.

I'm not sure why I'm still there. But I think it has to do with the fact that I have nowhere else to go. No one needs me and that's a little depressing. A part of me would like to have a girlfriend, but that involves a lot of energy and work. And, let's face it, I can barely handle getting up the stairs.

There was a serious girlfriend a long time ago, but it didn't last. At the time, I think I loved her, but things didn't work out and we went our separate ways. It was hard at the time, but nothing I couldn't get over. I've never had trouble attracting women. I think they like the broody, not interested vibes I give off. But, for whatever reason, I lose interest fast and nothing lasts past a couple of dates and a romp or two in the sheets.

My siblings are lucky, but I'm not sure it'll ever happen for me. Love is a strange thing, and no woman has ever had the power to sweep into my world and knock me off my feet. Honestly, I doubt the perfect woman even exists for me. Hell, even if I could make her up from scratch myself, I don't even know what I want. Blonde? Brunette? Short? Tall? Bubbly? Smart? Funny? Silly?

Eh. Who knows? I sure don't, so it's really not a surprise that no one is able to catch my attention for long.

I glance down at my watch, wondering where my brother is, then look up right as Luca's Mercedes pulls up behind my car. It's about time. Unzipping the case that holds my racket, I pull it out and stand up. Luca walks over and we bump knuckles.

"Your wife is already knocked up," I tease him good naturedly. "Give her a break, Jesus."

Luca laughs. "Yeah, right. I can't stay away from her. It's like she's a drug and I just want to be high on her all the time."

"That's a lovely analogy," I say dryly.

"Hey, I never claimed to be a poet."

There's a warm glow in his brown eyes and it appeared after he met Finley. My younger brother can turn on the charm, but now he saves it all for his wife. I used to be able to be charming, but now I can't be bothered. It takes too much energy and there's no woman I've met lately that makes me want to exert that kind of effort. Especially, when I'm so damn tired all the time.

Relationships are hard work and I have way too much on my plate right now. Or, so I try to tell myself.

"C'mon, old man," he says and bounces a ball with his racket. "I'm ready to beat your ass."

"Yeah, right. Not gonna happen."

We move to opposite ends of the tennis court and Luca tosses the ball up and slams it hard. I run forward and hit it back over the net. We go back and forth for a little bit until I miss, and Luca whoops it up.

Trying to ignore the intense beating of my heart, the flutters I'm feeling at the hollow of my throat, I shake my head and lift my middle finger. Once I'm back in position, knees bent, I spin my racket and keep my eyes on the ball. Luca serves and I race forward and slam my racket into the ball, sending it right back over the net and barreling over where Luca easily hits it back.

Shit. I hurry to reach the ball, but miss, and suddenly it feels like a freight train is running over my chest. With a gasp, I drop my racket, lean over and plant my hands on my knees, wheezing. Trying to catch my breath is beyond me at this point and I hear Luca calling my name.

It's the last thing I hear, too, because suddenly my knees buckle and I drop to the ground, my head hitting the hard pavement.

Read the complete story HERE!

SUBSCRIBE TO MY MAILING LIST

I hope you enjoyed reading this book.

In case you would like to receive information on my latest releases, price promotions, and any special giveaways, then I would recommend you to subscribe to my mailing list.

You can do so now by using the subscription link below.

SUBSCRIBE TO AVA GRAY's MAILING LIST!

Printed in Great Britain
by Amazon

38510354R00158